Sir Perceval of Galles

Anonymous

MythBank

This edition is Copyright © 2020 by Jason Hamilton

All rights reserved.

No original part of this book may be reproduced in any form or by any electronic or mechanical means, including information storage and retrieval systems, without written permission from the author. All short stories found therein are in the public domain.

MythBank

www.mythbank.com

Cover design by Jason Hamilton.

Contents

About MythBank   I

1. Sir Perceval of Galles   1

More Arthurian Legends   155

About MythBank

MythBank is a website devoted to the documentation and study of stories. As part of that initiative, this collection was created with the purpose of ensuring all public domain classics had attractive, uniform, and readily available print copies and ebooks.

Through print on demand, many classics that are lesser-known or have limited runs can still be available for anyone who wants it, keeping the price steady and reducing the need to search the dregs of used books for a copy that might cost ten times what it's worth.

We hope you enjoy this collection of classics and recommend you visit our website to learn more. Additionally, you will find other classics in this collection that are designed to match the same branding and tone of this volume, so they look amazing on your shelf or your device. Check them out!

Contents

About MythBank   I

1. Sir Perceval of Galles   1

More Arthurian Legends   155

About MythBank

MythBank is a website devoted to the documentation and study of stories. As part of that initiative, this collection was created with the purpose of ensuring all public domain classics had attractive, uniform, and readily available print copies and ebooks.

Through print on demand, many classics that are lesser-known or have limited runs can still be available for anyone who wants it, keeping the price steady and reducing the need to search the dregs of used books for a copy that might cost ten times what it's worth.

We hope you enjoy this collection of classics and recommend you visit our website to learn more. Additionally, you will find other classics in this collection that are designed to match the same branding and tone of this volume, so they look amazing on your shelf or your device. Check them out!

Sir Perceval of Galles

L EF, LYTHES TO ME
  Two wordes or thre,
Of one that was faire and fre
 And felle in his fighte.
His righte name was Percyvell,
He was fosterde in the felle,
He dranke water of the welle,
 And yitt was he wyghte.
His fadir was a noble man;
Fro the tyme that he began,
Miche wirchippe he wan
 When he was made knyghte
In Kyng Arthures haulle.
Beste byluffede of alle,
Percyvell thay gan hym calle,
 Whoso redis ryghte.

Who that righte can rede,
He was doughty of dede,
A styffe body on a stede
 Wapynes to welde;

Tharefore Kyng Arthoure
Dide hym mekill honoure:
He gaffe hym his syster Acheflour,
    To have and to holde
Fro thethyn till his lyves ende,
With brode londes to spende,
For he the knyght wele kende.
    He bytaughte hir to welde,
With grete gyftes to fulfill;
He gaffe his sister hym till
To the knyght, at ther bothers will,
    With robes in folde.

He gaffe hym robes in folde,
Brode londes in wolde,
Mony mobles untolde,
    His syster to take.
To the kirke the knyghte yode
For to wedde that frely fode,
For the gyftes that ware gude
    And for hir ownn sake.
Sythen, withowtten any bade,
A grete brydale thay made,
For hir sake that hym hade
    Chosen to hir make;
And after, withowtten any lett,
A grete justyng ther was sett;
Of all the kempes that he mett
    Wolde he none forsake.

Wolde he none forsake,

The Rede Knyghte ne the Blake,
Ne none that wolde to hym take
   With schafte ne with schelde;
He dose als a noble knyghte,
Wele haldes that he highte;
Faste preves he his myghte:
   Deres hym none elde.
Sexty schaftes, I say,
Sir Percyvell brake that ilke day,
And ever that riche lady lay
   One walle and byhelde.
Thofe the Rede Knyghte hade sworne,
Oute of his sadill is he borne
And almoste his lyfe forlorne,
   And lygges in the felde.

There he lygges in the felde -
Many men one hym byhelde -
Thurgh his armour and his schelde
   Stoneyde that tyde.
That arghede all that ther ware,
Bothe the lesse and the mare,
That noble Percyvell so wele dare
   Syche dynttys habyde.
Was ther nowthir more ne lasse
Of all those that ther was
That durste mete hym one the grasse,
   Agaynes hym to ryde.
Thay gaffe Sir Percyvell the gree:
Beste worthy was he;
And hamewardes than rode he,

And blythe was his bryde.

And thofe the bryde blythe be
That Percyvell hase wone the gree,
Yete the Rede Knyghte es he
   Hurte of his honde;
And therfore gyffes he a gyfte
That if he ever covere myghte
Owthir by day or by nyghte,
   In felde for to stonde,
That he scholde qwyte hym that dynt
That he of his handes hynte;
Sall never this travell be tynt,
   Ne tolde in the londe
That Percyvell in the felde
Schulde hym schende thus undire schelde,
Bot he scholde agayne it yelde,
   If that he were leveande.

Now than are thay leveande bathe;
Was noghte the Rede Knyghte so rathe
For to wayte hym with skathe.
   Er ther the harmes felle,
Ne befelle ther no stryffe,
Till Percyvell had in his lyffe
A son by his yonge wyffe,
   Aftir hym to duelle.
When the childe was borne,
He made calle it one the morne
Als his fadir highte byforne -
   Yonge Percyvell.

The knyghte was fayne a feste made
For knave-childe that he hade;
And sythen, withowtten any bade
　Offe justynges they telle.

Now of justynges they tell:
They sayne that Sir Percyvell
That he will in the felde duelle,
　Als he hase are done.
A grete justynge was ther sett
Of all the kempes that ther mett,
For he wolde his son were gette
　In the same wonne.
Theroff the Rede Knyghte was blythe,
When he herde of that justynge kythe,
And graythed hym armour ful swythe,
　And rode thedir righte sone;
Agayne Percyvell he rade,
With schafte and with schelde brade,
To holde his heste that he made,
　Of maistres to mone.

Now of maistres to mone,
Percyvell hase wele done,
For the love of his yonge sone,
　One the firste day.
Ere the Rede Knyghte was bownn,
Percyvell hase borne downn
Knyght, duke, erle, and baroun,
　And vencusede the play.
Right als he hade done this honour,

So come the Rede Knyghte to the stowre.

Bot "Wo worthe wykkyde armour!"

  Percyvell may say.

For ther was Sir Percyvell slayne,

And the Rede Knyghte fayne -

In herte is noghte for to layne -

  When he went on his way.

When he went on his way,

Durste ther no man to hym say,

Nowther in erneste ne in play,

  To byd hym habyde;

For he had slayne righte thare

The beste body at thare ware,

Sir Percyvell, with woundes sare,

  And stonayed that tyde.

And than thay couthe no better rede

Bot put hym in a prevee stede,

Als that men dose with the dede,

  In erthe for to hyde.

Scho that was his lady

Mighte be full sary,

That lorne hade siche a body:

  Hir aylede no pryde.

And now is Percyvell the wighte

Slayne in batelle and in fyghte,

And the lady hase gyffen a gyfte,

  Holde if scho may,

That scho schall never mare wone

In stede, with hir yonge sone,

Ther dedes of armes schall be done,
   By nyghte ne be daye.
Bot in the wodde schall he be:
Sall he no thyng see
Bot the leves of the tree
   And the greves graye;
Schall he nowther take tent
To justes ne to tournament,
Bot in the wilde wodde went,
   With bestes to playe.

With wilde bestes for to playe,
Scho tuke hir leve and went hir waye,
Bothe at baron and at raye,
   And went to the wodde.
Byhynde scho leved boure and haulle;
A mayden scho tuke hir withalle,
That scho myghte appon calle
   When that hir nede stode.
Other gudes wolde scho nonne nayte,
Bot with hir tuke a tryppe of gayte,
With mylke of tham for to bayte
   To hir lyves fode.
Off all hir lordes faire gere,
Wolde scho noghte with hir bere
Bot a lyttill Scottes spere,
   Agayne hir son yode.

And when hir yong son yode,
Scho bade hym walke in the wodde,
Tuke hym the Scottes spere gude,

And gaffe hym in hande.
"Swete modir," sayde he,
"What manere of thyng may this bee
That ye nowe hafe taken mee?
　What calle yee this wande?"
Than byspakke the lady:
"Son," scho sayde, "sekerly,
It es a dart doghty;
　In the wodde I it fande."
The childe es payed, of his parte,
His modir hafe gyffen hym that darte;
Therwith made he many marte
　In that wodde-lande.

Thus he welke in the lande,
With hys darte in his hande;
Under the wilde wodde-wande
　He wexe and wele thrafe.
He wolde schote with his spere
Bestes and other gere,
As many als he myghte bere.
　He was a gude knave!
Smalle birdes wolde he slo,
Hertys, hyndes also;
Broghte his moder of thoo:
　Thurte hir none crave.
So wele he lernede hym to schote,
Ther was no beste that welke one fote
To fle fro hym was it no bote.
　When that he wolde hym have,

Even when he wolde hym have.
Thus he wexe and wele thrave,
And was reghte a gude knave
 Within a fewe yere.
Fyftene wynter and mare
He duellede in those holtes hare;
Nowther nurture ne lare
 Scho wolde hym none lere.
Till it byfelle, on a day,
The lady till hir son gun say,
"Swete childe, I rede thou praye
 To Goddes Sone dere,
That he wolde helpe the -
Lorde, for His poustee -
A gude man for to bee,
 And longe to duelle here."

"Swete moder," sayde he,
"Whatkyns a godd may that be
That ye nowe bydd mee
 That I schall to pray?"
Then byspakke the lady even:
"It es the grete Godd of heven:
This worlde made He within seven,
 Appon the sexte day."
"By grete Godd," sayde he than,
"And I may mete with that man,
With alle the crafte that I kan,
 Reghte so schall I pray!"
There he levede in a tayte
Bothe his modir and his gayte,

The grete Godd for to layte,
   Fynde hym when he may.

And as he welke in holtes hare,
He sawe a gate, as it ware;
With thre knyghtis mett he thare
   Off Arthrus in.
One was Ewayne fytz Asoure,
Another was Gawayne with honour,
And Kay, the bolde baratour,
   And all were of his kyn.
In riche robes thay ryde;
The childe hadd no thyng that tyde
That he myghte in his bones hyde,
   Bot a gaytes skynn.
He was a burely of body, and therto right brade;
One ayther halfe a skynn he hade;
The hode was of the same made,
   Juste to the chynn.

His hode was juste to his chyn,
The flesche halfe tourned within.
The childes witt was full thyn
   When he scholde say oughte.
Thay were clothede all in grene;
Siche hade he never sene:
Wele he wened that thay had bene
   The Godd that he soghte.
He said, "Wilke of yow alle three
May the grete Godd bee
That my moder tolde mee,

That all this werlde wroghte?"
Bot than ansuerde Sir Gawayne
Faire and curtaisely agayne,
"Son, so Criste mote me sayne,
   For swilke are we noghte."

Than saide the fole one the filde,
Was comen oute of the woddes wilde,
To Gawayne that was meke and mylde
   And softe to ansuare,
"I sall sla yow all three
Bot ye smertly now telle mee
Whatkyns thynges that ye bee,
   Sen ye no goddes are."
Then ansuerde Sir Kay,
"Who solde we than say
That hade slayne us to-day
   In this holtis hare?"
At Kayes wordes wexe he tene:
Bot he a grete bukke had bene,
Ne hadd he stonde tham bytwene,
   He hade hym slayne thare.

Bot than said Gawayn to Kay,
"Thi prowde wordes pares ay;
I scholde wyn this childe with play,
   And thou wolde holde the still.
Swete son," than said he,
"We are knyghtis all thre;
With Kyng Arthoure duelle wee,
   That hovyn es on hyll."

Then said Percyvell the lyghte,
In gayte-skynnes that was dyghte,
"Will Kyng Arthoure make me knyghte,
    And I come hym till?"
Than saide Sir Gawayne righte thare,
"I kane gyffe the nane ansuare;
Bot to the Kynge I rede thou fare,
    To wete his awenn will!"

To wete than the Kynges will
Thare thay hoven yitt still;
The childe hase taken hym till
    For to wende hame.
And als he welke in the wodde,
He sawe a full faire stode
Offe coltes and of meres gude,
    Bot never one was tame;
And sone saide he, "Bi Seyne John,
Swilke thynges as are yone
Rade the knyghtes apone;
    Knewe I thaire name,
Als ever mote I thryffe or thee,
The moste of yone that I see
Smertly schall bere mee
    Till I come to my dame."

He saide, "When I come to my dame,
And I fynde hir at hame,
Scho will telle the name
    Off this ilke thynge."
The moste mere he thare see

Smertly overrynnes he,
And saide, "Thou sall bere me
  To-morne to the Kynge."
Kepes he no sadill-gere,
Bot stert up on the mere:
Hamewarde scho gun hym bere,
  Withowtten faylynge.
The lady was never more sore bygone.
Scho wiste never whare to wonne,
When scho wiste hir yonge sonne
  Horse hame brynge.

Scho saw hym horse hame brynge;
Scho wiste wele, by that thynge,
That the kynde wolde oute sprynge
  For thynge that be moughte.
Than als sone saide the lady,
"That ever solde I sorowe dry,
For love of thi body,
  That I hafe dere boghte!
Dere son," saide scho hym to,
"Thou wirkeste thiselfe mekill unroo,
What will thou with this mere do,
  That thou hase hame broghte?"
Bot the boye was never so blythe
Als when he herde the name kythe
Of the stode-mere stythe.
  Of na thyng than he roghte.

Now he calles hir a mere,
Als his moder dide ere;

He wened all other horses were
   And hade bene callede soo.
"Moder, at yonder hill hafe I bene;
Thare hafe I thre knyghtes sene,
And I hafe spoken with tham, I wene,
   Wordes in throo;
I have highte tham all thre
Before thaire Kyng for to be:
Siche on schall he make me
   As is one of tho!"
He sware by grete Goddes myghte,
"I schall holde that I hafe highte;
Bot-if the Kyng make me knyghte,
   To-morne I sall hym sloo!"

Bot than byspakke the lady,
That for hir son was sary -
Hir thoghte wele that scho myght dy
   And knelyde one hir knee:
"Sone, thou has takyn thi rede,
To do thiselfe to the dede!
In everilke a strange stede,
   Doo als I bydde the:
To-morne es forthirmaste Yole-day,
And thou says thou will away
To make the knyghte, if thou may,
   Als thou tolde mee.
Lyttill thou can of nurtoure:
Luke thou be of mesure
Bothe in haulle and in boure,
   And fonde to be fre."

Than saide the lady so brighte,
"There thou meteste with a knyghte,
Do thi hode off, I highte,
    And haylse hym in hy."
"Swete moder," sayd he then,
"I saw never yit no men;
If I solde a knyghte ken,
    Telles me wharby."
Scho schewede hym the menevaire -
Scho had robes in payre.
"Sone, ther thou sees this fare
    In thaire hodes lye."
"Bi grete God," sayd he,
"Where that I a knyghte see,
Moder, as ye bidd me,
    Righte so schall I."

All that nyghte till it was day,
The childe by the modir lay,
Till on the morne he wolde away,
    For thyng that myghte betyde.
Brydill hase he righte nane;
Seese he no better wane,
Bot a wythe hase he tane,
    And kevylles his stede.
His moder gaffe hym a ryng,
And bad he solde agayne it bryng;
"Sonne, this sall be oure takynnyng,
    For here I sall the byde."
He tase the rynge and the spere,

Stirttes up appon the mere:
Fro the moder that hym bere,
   Forthe gan he ryde.

One his way as he gan ryde,
He fande an haulle ther besyde;
He saide, "For oghte that may betyde,
   Thedir in will I."
He went in withowtten lett;
He fande a brade borde sett,
A bryghte fire, wele bett,
   Brynnande therby.
A mawnger ther he fande,
Corne therin lyggande;
Therto his mere he bande
   With the withy.
He saide, "My modir bad me
That I solde of mesure bee
Halfe that I here see
   Styll sall it ly."

The corne he pertis in two,
Gaffe his mere the tone of thoo,
And to the borde gan he goo,
   Certayne that tyde.
He fande a lofe of brede fyne
And a pychere with wyne,
A mese of the kechyne,
   A knyfe ther besyde.
The mete ther that he fande,
He dalte it even with his hande,

Lefte the halfe lyggande
  A felawe to byde.
The tother halfe ete he;
How myghte he more of mesure be?
Faste he fonded to be free,
  Thofe he were of no pryde.

Thofe he were of no pryde,
Forthyrmore gan he glyde
Till a chambir ther besyde,
  Moo sellys to see.
Riche clothes fande he sprede,
A lady slepande on a bedde;
He said, "Forsothe, a tokyn to wedde
  Sall thou lefe with mee."
Ther he kyste that swete thynge;
Of hir fynger he tuke a rynge;
His awenn modir takynnynge
  He lefte with that fre.
He went forthe to his mere,
Tuke with hym his schorte spere,
Lepe on lofte, as he was ere;
  His way rydes he.

Now on his way rydes he,
Moo selles to see;
A knyghte wolde he nedis bee,
  Withowtten any bade.
He came ther the Kyng was,
Servede of the firste mese.
To hym was the maste has

That the childe hade;
And thare made he no lett
At gate, dore, ne wykett,
Bot in graythely he gett -
    Syche maistres he made.
At his firste in-comynge,
His mere, withowtten faylynge,
Kyste the forhevede of the Kynge -
    So nerehande he rade!

The Kyng had ferly thaa,
And up his hande gan he taa
And putt it forthir hym fraa,
    The mouthe of the mere.
He saide, "Faire childe and free,
Stonde still besyde mee,
And tell me wythen that thou bee,
    And what thou will here."
Than said the fole of the filde,
"I ame myn awnn modirs childe,
Comen fro the woddes wylde
    Till Arthure the dere.
Yisterday saw I knyghtis three:
Siche on sall thou make mee
On this mere byfor the,
    Thi mete or thou schere!"

Bot than spak Sir Gawayne,
Was the Kynges trenchepayne,
Said, "Forsothe, is noghte to layne,
    I am one of thaa.

Childe, hafe thou my blyssyng
For thi feres folowynge!
Here hase thou fonden the Kynge
    That kan the knyghte maa."
Than sayde Peceyvell the free,
"And this Arthure the Kyng bee,
Luke he a knyghte make mee:
    I rede at it be swaa!"
Thofe he unborely were dyghte,
He sware by mekill Goddes myghte:
"Bot if the Kyng make me knyghte,
    I sall hym here slaa!"

All that ther weren, olde and yynge,
Hadden ferly of the Kyng,
That he wolde suffre siche a thyng
    Of that foull wyghte
On horse hovande hym by.
The Kyng byholdes hym on hy;
Than wexe he sone sory
    When he sawe that syghte.
The teres oute of his eghne glade,
Never one another habade.
"Allas," he sayde, "that I was made,
    Be day or by nyghte,
One lyve I scholde after hym bee
That me thynke lyke the: In the tyme of Arthur an aunter
bytydde,
    By the Turne Wathelan, as the boke telles,
    Whan he to Carlele was comen, that conquerour kydde,
    With dukes and dussiperes that with the dere dwelles.

To hunte at the herdes that longe had ben hydde,
On a day thei hem dight to the depe delles,
To fall of the femailes in forest were frydde,
Fayre by the fermesones in frithes and felles.
Thus to wode arn thei went, the wlonkest in wedes,
Bothe the Kyng and the Quene,
And al the doughti bydene.
Sir Gawayn, gayest on grene,
Dame Gaynour he ledes.

Thus Sir Gawayn the gay Gaynour he ledes,
In a gleterand gide that glemed full gay -
With riche ribaynes reversset, ho so right redes,
Rayled with rybees of riall array;
Her hode of a hawe huwe, ho that here hede hedes,
Of pillour, of palwerk, of perré to pay;
Schurde in a short cloke that the rayne shedes,
Set over with saffres sothely to say,
With saffres and seladynes set by the sides;
Here sadel sette of that ilke,
Saude with sambutes of silke;
On a mule as the mylke,
Gaili she glides.

Al in gleterand golde, gayly ho glides
The gates with Sir Gawayn, bi the grene welle.
And that burne on his blonke with the Quene bides
That borne was in Borgoyne, by boke and by belle.
He ladde that Lady so longe by the lawe sides;
Under a lorre they light, loghe by a felle.
And Arthur with his erles ernestly rides,

To teche hem to her tristres, the trouthe for to telle.
To here tristres he hem taught, ho the trouthe trowes.
Eche lorde withouten lette
To an oke he hem sette,
With bowe and with barselette,
Under the bowes.

Under the bowes thei bode, thes burnes so bolde,
To byker at thes baraynes in bonkes so bare.
There might hatheles in high herdes beholde,
Herken huntyng in hast, in holtes so hare.
Thei kest of here couples in cliffes so colde,
Conforte her kenettes to kele hem of care.
Thei fel of the femayles ful thikfolde;
With fressh houndes and fele, thei folowen her fare.
. . . .
With gret questes and quelles,
Both in frethes and felles.
All the dure in the delles,
Thei durken and dare.

Then durken the dere in the dymme skuwes,
That for drede of the deth droupes the do.
And by the stremys so strange that swftly swoghes
Thai werray the wilde and worchen hem wo.
The huntes thei halowe, in hurstes and huwes,
And till thaire riste raches relyes on the ro.
They gaf to no gamon grythe that on grounde gruwes.
The grete greundes in the greves so glady thei go;
So gladly thei gon in greves so grene.
The King blowe rechas

And folowed fast on the tras
With many sergeant of mas,
That solas to sene.

With solas thei semble, the pruddest in palle,
And suwen to the Soverayne within schaghes schene.
Al but Sir Gawayn, gayest of all,
Beleves with Dame Gaynour in greves so grene.
By a lorer ho was light, undur a lefesale
Of box and of berber bigged ful bene.
Fast byfore undre this ferly con fall
And this mekel mervaile that I shal of mene.
Now wol I of this mervaile mele, if I mote.
The day wex als dirke
As hit were mydnight myrke;
Thereof the King was irke
And light on his fote.

Thus to fote ar thei faren, the frekes unfayn,
And fleen fro the forest to the fawe felle.
Thay ranne faste to the roches, for reddoure of the raynne
For the sneterand snawe snartly hem snelles.
There come a lowe one the loughe - in londe is not to layne
In the lyknes of Lucyfere, laytheste in Helle,
And glides to Sir Gawayn the gates to gayne,
Yauland and yomerand, with many loude yelle.
Hit yaules, hit yameres, with waymynges wete,
And seid, with siking sare,
"I ban the body me bare!
Alas! Now kindeles my care;
I gloppen and I grete!"

Then gloppenet and grete Gaynour the gay
And seid to Sir Gawen, "What is thi good rede?"
"Hit ar the clippes of the son, I herd a clerk say,"
And thus he confortes the Quene for his knighthede.
"Sir Cadour, Sir Clegis, Sir Costardyne, Sir Cay -
Thes knyghtes arn uncurtays, by Crosse and by Crede,
That thus oonly have me laft on my dethday
With the grisselist goost that ever herd I grede."
"Of the goost," quod the grome, "greve you no mare,
For I shal speke with the sprete.
And of the wayes I shall wete,
What may the bales bete
Of the bodi bare."

Bare was the body and blak to the bone,
Al biclagged in clay uncomly cladde.
Hit waried, hit wayment as a woman,
But on hide ne on huwe no heling hit hadde.
Hit stemered, hit stonayde, hit stode as a stone,
Hit marred, hit memered, hit mused for madde.
Agayn the grisly goost Sir Gawayn is gone;
He rayked oute at a res, for he was never drad.
Drad was he never, ho so right redes.
On the chef of the cholle,
A pade pikes on the polle,
With eighen holked ful holle
That gloed as the gledes.

Al glowed as a glede the goste there ho glides,
Umbeclipped in a cloude of clethyng unclere,

Serkeled with serpentes all aboute the sides -
To tell the todes theron my tonge wer full tere.
The burne braides oute the bronde, and the body bides;
Therefor the chevalrous knight changed no chere.
The houndes highen to the holtes, and her hede hides,
For the grisly goost made a grym bere.
The grete greundes wer agast of the grym bere.
The birdes in the bowes,
That on the goost glowes,
Thei skryke in the skowes
That hatheles may here.

Hathelese might here, the hendeste in halle,
How chatered the cholle, the chaftis and the chynne.
Then conjured the knight - on Crist con he calle:
"As thou was crucifiged on Croys to clanse us of syn:
That thou sei me the sothe whether thou shalle,
And whi thou walkest thes wayes the wodes within."
"I was of figure and face fairest of alle,
Cristened and knowen with kinges in my kynne;
I have kinges in my kyn knowen for kene.
God has me geven of his grace
To dre my paynes in this place.
I am comen in this cace
To speke with your Quene.

"Quene was I somwile, brighter of browes
Then Berell or Brangwayn, thes burdes so bolde;
Of al gamen or gle that on grounde growes
Gretter then Dame Gaynour, of garson and golde,
Of palaies, of parkes, of pondes, of plowes,

Of townes, of toures, of tresour untolde,
Of castelles, of contreyes, of cragges, of clowes.
Now am I caught oute of kide to cares so colde;
Into care am I caught and couched in clay.
Lo, sir curtays kniyght,
How delfulle deth has me dight!
Lete me onys have a sight
Of Gaynour the gay."

After Gaynour the gay Sir Gawyn is gon,
And to the body he her brought, the burde bright.
"Welcom, Waynour, iwis, worthi in won.
Lo, how delful deth has thi dame dight!
I was radder of rode then rose in the ron,
My ler as the lelé lonched on hight.
Now am I a graceles gost, and grisly I gron;
With Lucyfer in a lake logh am I light.
Thus am I lyke to Lucefere: takis witnes by mee!
For al thi fressh foroure,
Muse on my mirrour;
For, king and emperour,
Thus dight shul ye be.

"Thus dethe wil you dight, thare you not doute;
Thereon hertly take hede while thou art here.
Whan thou art richest arraied and ridest in thi route,
Have pité on the poer - thou art of power.
Burnes and burdes that ben the aboute,
When thi body is bamed and brought on a ber,
Then lite wyn the light that now wil the loute,
For then the helpes no thing but holy praier.

The praier of poer may purchas the pes -
Of that thou yeves at the yete,
Whan thou art set in thi sete,
With al merthes at mete
And dayntés on des.

"With riche dayntés on des thi diotes ar dight,
And I, in danger and doel, in dongone I dwelle,
Naxte and nedefull, naked on night.
Ther folo me a ferde of fendes of helle;
They hurle me unhendely; thei harme me in hight;
In bras and in brymston I bren as a belle.
Was never wrought in this world a wofuller wight.
Hit were ful tore any tonge my turment to telle;
Nowe wil Y of my turment tel or I go.
Thenk hertly on this -
Fonde to mende thi mys.
Thou art warned ywys:
Be war be my wo."

"Wo is me for thi wo," quod Waynour, "ywys!
But one thing wold I wite, if thi wil ware:
If auther matens or Mas might mende thi mys,
Or eny meble on molde? My merthe were the mare
If bedis of bisshopps might bring the to blisse,
Or coventes in cloistre might kere the of care.
If thou be my moder, grete mervaile hit is
That al thi burly body is broughte to be so bare!"
"I bare the of my body; what bote is hit I layn?
I brak a solempne avowe,
And no man wist hit but thowe;

By that token thou trowe,
That sothely I sayn."

"Say sothely what may the saven of thi sytis
And I shal make sere men to singe for thi sake.
But the baleful bestes that on thi body bites
Al blendis my ble - thi bones arn so blake!"
"That is luf paramour, listes and delites
That has me light and laft logh in a lake.
Al the welth of the world, that awey witis
With the wilde wormes that worche me wrake;
Wrake thei me worchen, Waynour, iwys.
Were thritty trentales don
Bytwene under and non,
Mi soule were socoured with son
And brought to the blys."

"To blisse bring the the Barne that bought the on Rode,
That was crucifiged on Croys and crowned with thorne.
As thou was cristened and crisomed with candel and code,
Folowed in fontestone on frely byforne -
Mary the mighti, myldest of mode,
Of whom the blisful barne in Bedlem was borne,
Lene me grace that I may grete the with gode
And mynge the with matens and Masses on morne."
"To mende us with Masses, grete myster hit were.
For Him that rest on the Rode,
Gyf fast of thi goode
To folke that failen the fode
While thou art here."

"Here hertly my honde thes hestes to holde,
With a myllion of Masses to make the mynnyng.
Bot one word," quod Waynour, "yit weten I wolde:
What wrathed God most, at thi weting?"
"Pride with the appurtenaunce, as prophetez han tolde
Bifore the peple, apertly in her preching.
Hit beres bowes bitter: therof be thou bolde;
That makes burnes so boune to breke his bidding.
But ho his bidding brekes, bare thei ben of blys;
But thei be salved of that sare,
Er they hethen fare,
They mon weten of care,
Waynour, ywys."

"Wysse me," quod Waynour, "som wey, if thou wost,
What bedis might me best to the blisse bring?"
"Mekenesse and mercy, thes arn the moost;
And sithen have pité on the poer, that pleses Heven king.
Sithen charité is chef, and then is chaste,
And then almessedede aure al other thing.
Thes arn the graceful giftes of the Holy Goste
That enspires iche sprete withoute speling.
Of this spiritual thing spute thou no mare.
Als thou art Quene in thi quert,
Hold thes wordes in hert.
Thou shal leve but a stert;
Hethen shal thou fare."

"How shal we fare," quod the freke, "that fonden to fight,
And thus defoulen the folke on fele kinges londes,
And riches over reymes withouten eny right,

Wynnen worshipp in werre thorgh wightnesse of hondes?"
"Your King is to covetous, I warne the sir knight.
May no man stry him with strenght while his whele stondes.
Whan he is in his magesté, moost in his might,
He shal light ful lowe on the sesondes.
And this chivalrous Kinge chef shall a chaunce:
Falsely Fortune in fight,
That wonderfull wheelwryght,
Shall make lordes to light -
Take witnesse by Fraunce.

"Fraunce haf ye frely with your fight wonnen;
Freol and his folke, fey ar they leved.
Bretayne and Burgoyne al to you bowen,
And al the Dussiperes of Fraunce with your dyn deved.
Gyan may grete the werre was bigonen;
There ar no lordes on lyve in that londe leved.
Yet shal the riche Romans with you be aurronen,
And with the Rounde Table the rentes be reved;
Then shal a Tyber untrue tymber you tene.
Gete the, Sir Gawayn:
Turne the to Tuskayn.
For ye shul lese Bretayn
With a knight kene.

"This knight shal kenely croyse the crowne,
And at Carlele shal that comly be crowned as king.
That sege shal be sesede at a sesone
That myche baret and bale to Bretayn shal bring.
Hit shal in Tuskan be tolde of the treson,
And ye shullen turne ayen for the tydynge.

Ther shal the Rounde Table lese the renoune:
Beside Ramsey ful rad at a riding
In Dorsetshire shal dy the doughtest of alle.
Gete the, Sir Gawayn,
The boldest of Bretayne;
In a slake thou shal be slayne,
Sich ferlyes shull falle.

"Suche ferlies shull fal, withoute eny fable,
Uppon Cornewayle coost with a knight kene.
Sir Arthur the honest, avenant and able,
He shal be wounded, iwys - wothely, I wene.
And al the rial rowte of the Rounde Table,
Thei shullen dye on a day, the doughty bydene,
Suppriset with a suget: he beris hit in sable,
With a sauter engreled of silver full shene.
He beris hit of sable, sothely to say;
In riche Arthures halle,
The barne playes at the balle
That outray shall you alle,
Delfully that day.

"Have gode day, Gaynour, and Gawayn the gode;
I have no lenger tome tidinges to telle.
I mot walke on my wey thorgh this wilde wode
In my wonyngstid in wo for to welle.
Fore Him that rightwisly rose and rest on the Rode,
Thenke on the danger and the dole that I yn dwell.
Fede folke for my sake that failen the fode
And menge me with matens and Masse in melle.
Masses arn medecynes to us that bale bides;

Us thenke a Masse as swete
As eny spice that ever ye yete."
With a grisly grete
The goste awey glides.

With a grisly grete the goost awey glides
And goes with gronyng sore thorgh the greves grene.
The wyndes, the weders, the welken unhides -
Then unclosed the cloudes, the son con shene.
The King his bugle has blowen and on the bent bides;
His fare folke in the frith, thei flokken bydene,
And al the riall route to the Quene rides;
She sayes hem the selcouthes that thei hadde ther seen.
The wise of the weder, forwondred they were.
Prince proudest in palle,
Dame Gaynour and alle,
Went to Rondoles Halle
To the suppere.

The King to souper is set, served in sale,
Under a siller of silke dayntly dight
With al worshipp and wele, innewith the walle,
Briddes brauden and brad in bankers bright.
There come in a soteler with a symballe,
A lady lufsom of lote ledand a knight;
Ho raykes up in a res bifor the Rialle
And halsed Sir Arthur hendly on hight.
Ho said to the Soverayne, wlonkest in wede,
"Mon makeles of might,
Here commes an errant knight.
Do him reson and right

For thi manhede."

The mon in his mantell sittes at his mete
In pal pured to pay, prodly pight,
Trofelyte and traverste with trewloves in trete;
The tasses were of topas that wer thereto tight.
He gliffed up with his eighen that grey wer and grete,
With his beveren berde, on that burde bright.
He was the soveraynest of al sitting in sete
That ever segge had sen with his eye sight.
King crowned in kith carpes hir tille:
"Welcom, worthely wight -
He shal have reson and right!
Whethen is the comli knight,
If hit be thi wille?"

Ho was the worthiest wight that eny wy welde wolde;
Here gide was glorious and gay, of a gresse grene.
Here belle was of blunket, with birdes ful bolde,
Brauded with brende gold, and bokeled ful bene.
Here fax in fyne perré was fretted in folde,
Contrefelet and kelle coloured full clene,
With a crowne craftly al of clene golde.
Here kercheves were curiouse with many proude prene,
Her perré was praysed with prise men of might:
Bright birdes and bolde
Had ynoghe to beholde
Of that frely to folde,
And on the hende knight.

The knight in his colours was armed ful clene,

With his comly crest clere to beholde,
His brené and his basnet burneshed ful bene,
With a bordur abought al of brende golde.
His mayles were mylke white, enclawet ful clene;
His horse trapped of that ilke, as true men me tolde;
His shelde on his shulder of silver so shene,
With bere hedes of blake browed ful bolde;
His horse in fyne sandel was trapped to the hele.
And, in his cheveron biforne,
Stode as an unicorne,
Als sharp as a thorne,
An anlas of stele.

In stele he was stuffed, that stourne uppon stede,
Al of sternes of golde, that stanseld was one straye;
His gloves, his gamesons glowed as a glede
With graynes of rebé that graithed ben gay.
And his schene schynbaudes, that sharp wer to shrede,
His poleinus with pelydodis were poudred to pay.
With a launce on loft that lovely con lede;
A freke on a freson him folowed, in fay.
The freson was afered for drede of that fare,
For he was selden wonte to se
The tablet fluré:
Siche gamen ne gle
Sagh he never are.

Arthur asked on hight, herand him alle:
"What woldes thou, wee, if hit be thi wille?
Tel me what thou seches and whether thou shalle,
And whi thou, sturne on thi stede, stondes so stille?"

He wayved up his viser fro his ventalle;
With a knightly contenaunce, he carpes him tille:
"Whether thou be cayser or king, her I the becalle
Fore to finde me a freke to fight with my fille.
Fighting to fraist I fonded fro home."
Then seid the King uppon hight,
"If thou be curteys knight,
Late and lenge al nyght,
And tel me thi nome."

"Mi name is Sir Galaron, withouten eny gile,
The grettest of Galwey of greves and gyllis,
Of Connok, of Conyngham, and also Kyle,
Of Lomond, of Losex, of Loyan hilles.
Thou has wonen hem in werre with a wrange wile
And geven hem to Sir Gawayn - that my hert grylles.
But he shal wring his honde and warry the wyle,
Er he weld hem, ywys, agayn myn unwylles.
Bi al the welth of the worlde, he shal hem never welde,
While I the hede may bere,
But if he wyn hem in were,
With a shelde and a spere,
On a faire felde.

"I wol fight on a felde - thereto I make feith -
With eny freke uppon folde that frely is borne.
To lese suche a lordshipp me wolde thenke laith,
And iche lede opon lyve wold lagh me to scorne."
"We ar in the wode went to walke on oure waith,
To hunte at the hertes with hounde and with horne.
We ar in oure gamen; we have no gome graithe,

But yet thou shalt be mached be mydday tomorne.
Forthi I rede the, thenke rest al night."
Gawayn, grathest of all,
Ledes him oute of the hall
Into a pavilion of pall
That prodly was pight.

Pight was it prodly with purpour and palle,
Birdes brauden above, in brend gold bright.
Inwith was a chapell, a chambour, a halle,
A chymné with charcole to chaufe the knight.
His stede was stabled and led to the stalle;
Hay hertly he had in haches on hight.
Sithen thei braide up a borde, and clothes thei calle,
Sanapes and salers, semly to sight,
Torches and brochetes and stondardes bitwene.
Thus thei served that knight
And his worthely wight,
With rich dayntes dight
In silver so shene.

In silver so semely thei served of the best,
With vernage in veres and cuppes ful clene.
And thus Sir Gawayn the good glades hour gest,
With riche dayntees endored in disshes bydene.
Whan the riall renke was gone to his rest,
The King to counsaile has called his knightes so kene.
"Loke nowe, lordes, oure lose be not lost.
Ho shal encontre with the knight? Kestes you bitwene."
Then seid Gawayn the goode, "Shal hit not greve.
Here my honde I you hight,

I woll fight with the knight
In defence of my right,
Lorde, by your leve."

"I leve wel," quod the King. "Thi lates ar light,
But I nolde for no lordeshipp se thi life lorne."
"Let go!" quod Sir Gawayn. "God stond with the right!
If he skape skathlesse, hit were a foule skorne."
In the daying of the day, the doughti were dight,
And herden matens and Masse erly on morne.
By that on Plumton Land a palais was pight,
Were never freke opon folde had foughten biforne.
Thei setten listes bylyve on the logh lande.
Thre soppes demayn
Thei brought to Sir Gawayn
For to confort his brayn,
The King gared commaunde.

The King commaunded kindeli the Erlis son of Kent:
"Curtaysly in this case, take kepe to the knight."
With riche dayntees or day he dyned in his tente;
After buskes him in a brené that burneshed was bright.
Sithen to Waynour wisly he went;
He laft in here warde his worthly wight.
After aither in high hour horses thei hent,
And at the listes on the lande lordely done light
Alle bot thes two burnes, baldest of blode.
The Kinges chaier is set
Abowve on a chacelet;
Many galiard gret
For Gawayn the gode.

Gawayn and Galerone gurden her stedes;
Al in gleterand golde, gay was here gere.
The lordes bylyve hom to list ledes,
With many serjant of mace, as was the manere.
The burnes broched the blonkes that the side bledis;
Ayther freke opon folde has fastned his spere.
Shaftes in shide wode thei shindre in shedes,
So jolilé thes gentil justed on were!
Shaftes thei shindre in sheldes so shene,
And sithen, with brondes bright,
Riche mayles thei right.
There encontres the knight
With Gawayn on grene.

Gawayn was gaily grathed in grene,
With his griffons of golde engreled full gay,
Trifeled with tranes and trueloves bitwene;
On a startand stede he strikes on stray.
That other in his turnaying, he talkes in tene:
"Whi drawes thou the on dregh and makes siche deray?"
He swapped him yn at the swyre with a swerde kene;
That greved Sir Gawayn to his dethday.
The dyntes of that doughty were doutwis bydene;
Fifté mayles and mo
The swerde swapt in two,
The canelbone also,
And clef his shelde shene.

He clef thorgh the cantell that covered the knight,
Thorgh the shinand shelde a shaftmon and mare.

And then the lathely lord lowe uppon hight,
And Gawayn greches therwith and gremed ful sare:
"I shal rewarde the thi route, if I con rede right."
He folowed in on the freke with a fressh fare;
Thorgh blason and brené, that burneshed wer bright,
With a burlich bronde thorgh him he bare.
The bronde was blody that burneshed was bright.
Then gloppened that gay -
Hit was no ferly, in fay.
The sturne strikes on stray
In stiropes stright.

Streyte in his steroppes, stoutely he strikes,
And waynes at Sir Wawayn als he were wode.
Then his lemman on lowde skirles and skrikes,
When that burly burne blenket on blode.
Lordes and ladies of that laike likes
And thonked God of his grace for Gawayn the gode.
With a swap of a swerde, that swithely him swykes;
He stroke of the stede hede streite there he stode.
The faire fole fondred and fel, bi the Rode.
Gawayn gloppened in hert;
He was swithely smert.
Oute of sterops he stert
Fro Grissell the goode.

"Grissell," quod Gawayn, "gon is, God wote!
He was the burlokest blonke that ever bote brede.
By Him that in Bedeleem was borne ever to ben our bote,
I shall venge the today, if I con right rede."
"Go fecche me my freson, fairest on fote;

He may stonde the in stoure in as mekle stede."
"No more for the faire fole then for a risshrote.
But for doel of the dombe best that thus shuld be dede,
I mourne for no montur, for I may gete mare."
Als he stode by his stede,
That was so goode at nede,
Ner Gawayn wax wede,
So wepputte he sare.

Thus wepus for wo Wowayn the wight,
And wenys him to quyte, that wonded is sare.
That other drogh him on dreght for drede of the knight
And boldely broched his blonk on the bent bare.
"Thus may thou dryve forthe the day to the derk night!"
The son was passed by that mydday and mare.
Within the listes the lede lordly done light;
Touard the burne with his bronde he busked him yare.
To bataile they bowe with brondes so bright.
Shene sheldes wer shred,
Bright brenés bybled;
Many doughti were adred,
So fersely thei fight.

Thus thei feght on fote on that fair felde
As fressh as a lyon that fautes the fille.
Wilelé thes wight men thair wepenes they welde;
Wyte ye wele, Sir Gawayn wantis no will.
He brouched him yn with his bronde under the brode shelde
Thorgh the waast of the body and wonded him ille.
The swerd stent for no stuf - hit was so wel steled.
That other startis on bak and stondis stonstille.

Though he were stonayed that stonde, he strikes ful sare -
He gurdes to Sir Gawayn
Thorgh ventaile and pesayn;
He wanted noght to be slayn
The brede of an hare.

Hardely then thes hathelese on helmes they hewe.
Thei beten downe beriles and bourdures bright;
Shildes on shildres that shene were to shewe,
Fretted were in fyne golde, thei failen in fight.
Stones of iral thay strenkel and strewe;
Stithe stapeles of stele they strike done stright.
Burnes bannen the tyme the bargan was brewe,
The doughti with dyntes so delfully were dight.
The dyntis of tho doghty were doutous bydene.
Bothe Sir Lete and Sir Lake
Miche mornyng thei make.
Gaynor gret for her sake
With her grey eyen.

Thus gretis Gaynour with bothe her grey yene
For gref of Sir Gawayn, grisly was wound.
The knight of corage was cruel and kene,
And, with a stele bronde, that sturne oft stound;
Al the cost of the knyght he carf downe clene.
Thorgh the riche mailes that ronke were and rounde
With a teneful touche he taght him in tene,
He gurdes Sir Galeron groveling on gronde.
Grisly on gronde, he groned on grene.
Als wounded as he was,
Sone unredely he ras

And folowed fast on his tras
With a swerde kene.

Kenely that cruel kevered on hight,
And with a cast of the carhonde in cantil he strikes,
And waynes at Sir Wawyn, that worthely wight.
But him lymped the worse, and that me wel likes.
He atteled with a slenk haf slayn him in slight;
The swerd swapped on his swange and on the mayle slikes,
And Gawayn bi the coler keppes the knight.
Then his lemman on loft skrilles and skrikes -
Ho gretes on Gaynour with gronyng grylle:
"Lady makeles of might,
Haf mercy on yondre knight
That is so delfull dight,
If hit be thi wille."

Than wilfully Dame Waynour to the King went;
Ho caught of her coronall and kneled him tille:
"As thou art Roye roial, richest of rent,
And I thi wife wedded at thi owne wille -
Thes burnes in the bataile so blede on the bent,
They arn wery, iwis, and wonded full ille.
Thorgh her shene sheldes, her shuldres ar shent;
The grones of Sir Gawayn dos my hert grille.
The grones of Sir Gawayne greven me sare.
Wodest thou leve, Lorde,
Make thes knightes accorde,
Hit were a grete conforde
For all that here ware."

Then spak Sir Galeron to Gawayn the good:
"I wende never wee in this world had ben half so wight.
Here I make the releyse, renke, by the Rode,
And, byfore thiese ryalle, resynge the my ryghte;
And sithen make the monraden with a mylde mode
As man of medlert makeles of might."
He talkes touard the King on hie ther he stode,
And bede that burly his bronde that burneshed was bright:
"Of rentes and richesse I make the releyse."
Downe kneled the knight
And carped wordes on hight;
The King stode upright
And commaunded pes.

The King commaunded pes and cried on hight,
And Gawayn was goodly and laft for his sake.
Then lordes to listes they lopen ful light -
Sir Ewayn Fiz Uryayn and Arrak Fiz Lake,
Marrake and Moylard, that most wer of might -
Bothe thes travayled men they truly up take.
Unneth might tho sturne stonde upright -
What, for buffetes and blode, her blees wex blak;
Her blees were brosed, for beting of brondes.
Withouten more lettyng,
Dight was here saghtlyng;
Bifore the comly King,
Thei held up her hondes.

"Here I gif Sir Gawayn, with gerson and golde,
Al the Glamergan londe with greves so grene,
The worship of Wales at wil and at wolde,

With Criffones Castelles curnelled ful clene;
Eke Ulstur Halle to hafe and to holde,
Wayford and Waterforde, wallede I wene;
Two baronrees in Bretayne with burghes so bolde,
That arn batailed abought and bigged ful bene.
I shal doue the a duke and dubbe the with honde,
Withthi thou saghtil with the knight
That is so hardi and wight,
And relese him his right,
And graunte him his londe."

"Here I gif Sir Galeron," quod Gawayn, "withouten any gile,
Al the londes and the lithes fro Lauer to Layre,
Connoke and Carlele, Conyngham and Kile;
Yet, if he of chevalry chalange ham for aire,
The Lother, the Lemmok, the Loynak, the Lile,
With frethis and forestes and fosses so faire.
Withthi under our lordeship thou lenge here a while,
And to the Round Table make thy repaire,
I shal refeff the in felde in forestes so fair."
Bothe the King and the Quene
And al the doughti bydene,
Thorgh the greves so grene,
To Carlele thei cair.

The King to Carlele is comen with knightes so kene,
And al the Rounde Table on rial aray.
The wees that weren wounded so wothely, I wene,
Surgenes sone saned, sothely to say;
Bothe confortes the knightes, the King and the Quene.
Thei were dubbed dukes both on a day.

There he wedded his wife, wlonkest I wene,

With giftes and garsons, Sir Galeron the gay;

Thus that hathel in high withholdes that hende.

Whan he was saned sonde,

Thei made Sir Galeron that stonde

A knight of the Table Ronde

To his lyves ende.

Waynour gared wisely write into the west

To al the religious to rede and to singe;

Prestes with procession to pray were prest,

With a mylion of Masses to make the mynnynge.

Bokelered men, bisshops the best,

Thorgh al Bretayne belles the burde gared rynge.

This ferely bifelle in Ingulwud Forest,

Under a holte so hore at a huntyng -

Suche a huntyng in holtis is noght to be hide.

Thus to forest they fore,

Thes sterne knightes in store.

In the tyme of Arthore

This anter betide.In the tyme of Arthur an aunter bytydde,

By the Turne Wathelan, as the boke telles,

Whan he to Carlele was comen, that conquerour kydde,

With dukes and dussiperes that with the dere dwelles.

To hunte at the herdes that longe had ben hydde,

On a day thei hem dight to the depe delles,

To fall of the femailes in forest were frydde,

Fayre by the fermesones in frithes and felles.

Thus to wode arn thei went, the wlonkest in wedes,

Bothe the Kyng and the Quene,

And al the doughti bydene.

Sir Gawayn, gayest on grene,
Dame Gaynour he ledes.

Thus Sir Gawayn the gay Gaynour he ledes,
In a gleterand gide that glemed full gay -
With riche ribaynes reversset, ho so right redes,
Rayled with rybees of riall array;
Her hode of a hawe huwe, ho that here hede hedes,
Of pillour, of palwerk, of perré to pay;
Schurde in a short cloke that the rayne shedes,
Set over with saffres sothely to say,
With saffres and seladynes set by the sides;
Here sadel sette of that ilke,
Saude with sambutes of silke;
On a mule as the mylke,
Gaili she glides.

Al in gleterand golde, gayly ho glides
The gates with Sir Gawayn, bi the grene welle.
And that burne on his blonke with the Quene bides
That borne was in Borgoyne, by boke and by belle.
He ladde that Lady so longe by the lawe sides;
Under a lorre they light, loghe by a felle.
And Arthur with his erles ernestly rides,
To teche hem to her tristres, the trouthe for to telle.
To here tristres he hem taught, ho the trouthe trowes.
Eche lorde withouten lette
To an oke he hem sette,
With bowe and with barselette,
Under the bowes.

Under the bowes thei bode, thes burnes so bolde,
To byker at thes baraynes in bonkes so bare.
There might hatheles in high herdes beholde,
Herken huntyng in hast, in holtes so hare.
Thei kest of here couples in cliffes so colde,
Conforte her kenettes to kele hem of care.
Thei fel of the femayles ful thikfolde;
With fressh houndes and fele, thei folowen her fare.
. . . .
With gret questes and quelles,
Both in frethes and felles.
All the dure in the delles,
Thei durken and dare.

Then durken the dere in the dymme skuwes,
That for drede of the deth droupes the do.
And by the stremys so strange that swftly swoghes
Thai werray the wilde and worchen hem wo.
The huntes thei halowe, in hurstes and huwes,
And till thaire riste raches relyes on the ro.
They gaf to no gamon grythe that on grounde gruwes.
The grete greundes in the greves so glady thei go;
So gladly thei gon in greves so grene.
The King blowe rechas
And folowed fast on the tras
With many sergeant of mas,
That solas to sene.

With solas thei semble, the pruddest in palle,
And suwen to the Soverayne within schaghes schene.
Al but Sir Gawayn, gayest of all,

Beleves with Dame Gaynour in greves so grene."
By a lorer ho was light, undur a lefesale
Of box and of berber bigged ful bene.
Fast byfore undre this ferly con fall
And this mekel mervaile that I shal of mene.
Now wol I of this mervaile mele, if I mote.
The day wex als dirke
As hit were mydnight myrke;
Thereof the King was irke
And light on his fote.

Thus to fote ar thei faren, the frekes unfayn,
And fleen fro the forest to the fawe felle.
Thay ranne faste to the roches, for reddoure of the raynne
For the sneterand snawe snartly hem snelles.
There come a lowe one the loughe - in londe is not to layne -
In the lyknes of Lucyfere, laytheste in Helle,
And glides to Sir Gawayn the gates to gayne,
Yauland and yomerand, with many loude yelle.
Hit yaules, hit yameres, with waymynges wete,
And seid, with siking sare,
"I ban the body me bare!
Alas! Now kindeles my care;
I gloppen and I grete!"

Then gloppenet and grete Gaynour the gay
And seid to Sir Gawen, "What is thi good rede?"
"Hit ar the clippes of the son, I herd a clerk say,"
And thus he confortes the Quene for his knighthede.
"Sir Cadour, Sir Clegis, Sir Costardyne, Sir Cay -
Thes knyghtes arn uncurtays, by Crosse and by Crede,

That thus oonly have me laft on my dethday
With the grisselist goost that ever herd I grede."
"Of the goost," quod the grome, "greve you no mare,
For I shal speke with the sprete.
And of the wayes I shall wete,
What may the bales bete
Of the bodi bare."

Bare was the body and blak to the bone,
Al biclagged in clay uncomly cladde.
Hit waried, hit wayment as a woman,
But on hide ne on huwe no heling hit hadde.
Hit stemered, hit stonayde, hit stode as a stone,
Hit marred, hit memered, hit mused for madde.
Agayn the grisly goost Sir Gawayn is gone;
He rayked oute at a res, for he was never drad.
Drad was he never, ho so right redes.
On the chef of the cholle,
A pade pikes on the polle,
With eighen holked ful holle
That gloed as the gledes.

Al glowed as a glede the goste there ho glides,
Umbeclipped in a cloude of clethyng unclere,
Serkeled with serpentes all aboute the sides -
To tell the todes theron my tonge wer full tere.
The burne braides oute the bronde, and the body bides;
Therefor the chevalrous knight changed no chere.
The houndes highen to the holtes, and her hede hides,
For the grisly goost made a grym bere.
The grete greundes wer agast of the grym bere.

The birdes in the bowes,
That on the goost glowes,
Thei skryke in the skowes
That hatheles may here.

Hathelese might here, the hendeste in halle,
How chatered the cholle, the chaftis and the chynne.
Then conjured the knight - on Crist con he calle:
"As thou was crucifiged on Croys to clanse us of syn:
That thou sei me the sothe whether thou shalle,
And whi thou walkest thes wayes the wodes within."
"I was of figure and face fairest of alle,
Cristened and knowen with kinges in my kynne;
I have kinges in my kyn knowen for kene.
God has me geven of his grace
To dre my paynes in this place.
I am comen in this cace
To speke with your Quene.

"Quene was I somwile, brighter of browes
Then Berell or Brangwayn, thes burdes so bolde;
Of al gamen or gle that on grounde growes
Gretter then Dame Gaynour, of garson and golde,
Of palaies, of parkes, of pondes, of plowes,
Of townes, of toures, of tresour untolde,
Of castelles, of contreyes, of cragges, of clowes.
Now am I caught oute of kide to cares so colde;
Into care am I caught and couched in clay.
Lo, sir curtays kniyght,
How delfulle deth has me dight!
Lete me onys have a sight

Of Gaynour the gay."

After Gaynour the gay Sir Gawyn is gon,
And to the body he her brought, the burde bright.
"Welcom, Waynour, iwis, worthi in won.
Lo, how delful deth has thi dame dight!
I was radder of rode then rose in the ron,
My ler as the lelé lonched on hight.
Now am I a graceles gost, and grisly I gron;
With Lucyfer in a lake logh am I light.
Thus am I lyke to Lucefere: takis witnes by mee!
For al thi fressh foroure,
Muse on my mirrour;
For, king and emperour,
Thus dight shul ye be.

"Thus dethe wil you dight, thare you not doute;
Thereon hertly take hede while thou art here.
Whan thou art richest arraied and ridest in thi route,
Have pité on the poer - thou art of power.
Burnes and burdes that ben the aboute,
When thi body is bamed and brought on a ber,
Then lite wyn the light that now wil the loute,
For then the helpes no thing but holy praier.
The praier of poer may purchas the pes -
Of that thou yeves at the yete,
Whan thou art set in thi sete,
With al merthes at mete
And dayntés on des.

"With riche dayntés on des thi diotes ar dight,

And I, in danger and doel, in dongone I dwelle,
Naxte and nedefull, naked on night.
Ther folo me a ferde of fendes of helle;
They hurle me unhendely; thei harme me in hight;
In bras and in brymston I bren as a belle.
Was never wrought in this world a wofuller wight.
Hit were ful tore any tonge my turment to telle;
Nowe wil Y of my turment tel or I go.
Thenk hertly on this -
Fonde to mende thi mys.
Thou art warned ywys:
Be war be my wo."

"Wo is me for thi wo," quod Waynour, "ywys!
But one thing wold I wite, if thi wil ware:
If auther matens or Mas might mende thi mys,
Or eny meble on molde? My merthe were the mare
If bedis of bisshopps might bring the to blisse,
Or coventes in cloistre might kere the of care.
If thou be my moder, grete mervaile hit is
That al thi burly body is broughte to be so bare!"
"I bare the of my body; what bote is hit I layn?
I brak a solempne avowe,
And no man wist hit but thowe;
By that token thou trowe,
That sothely I sayn."

"Say sothely what may the saven of thi sytis
And I shal make sere men to singe for thi sake.
But the baleful bestes that on thi body bites
Al blendis my ble - thi bones arn so blake!"

"That is luf paramour, listes and delites
That has me light and laft logh in a lake.
Al the welth of the world, that awey witis
With the wilde wormes that worche me wrake;
Wrake thei me worchen, Waynour, iwys.
Were thritty trentales don
Bytwene under and non,
Mi soule were socoured with son
And brought to the blys."

"To blisse bring the the Barne that bought the on Rode,
That was crucifiged on Croys and crowned with thorne.
As thou was cristened and crisomed with candel and code,
Folowed in fontestone on frely byforne -
Mary the mighti, myldest of mode,
Of whom the blisful barne in Bedlem was borne,
Lene me grace that I may grete the with gode
And mynge the with matens and Masses on morne."
"To mende us with Masses, grete myster hit were.
For Him that rest on the Rode,
Gyf fast of thi goode
To folke that failen the fode
While thou art here."

"Here hertly my honde thes hestes to holde,
With a myllion of Masses to make the mynnyng.
Bot one word," quod Waynour, "yit weten I wolde:
What wrathed God most, at thi weting?"
"Pride with the appurtenaunce, as prophetez han tolde
Bifore the peple, apertly in her preching.
Hit beres bowes bitter: therof be thou bolde;

That makes burnes so boune to breke his bidding.
But ho his bidding brekes, bare thei ben of blys;
But thei be salved of that sare,
Er they hethen fare,
They mon weten of care,
Waynour, ywys."

"Wysse me," quod Waynour, "som wey, if thou wost,
What bedis might me best to the blisse bring?"
"Mekenesse and mercy, thes arn the moost;
And sithen have pité on the poer, that pleses Heven king.
Sithen charité is chef, and then is chaste,
And then almessedede aure al other thing.
Thes arn the graceful giftes of the Holy Goste
That enspires iche sprete withoute speling.
Of this spiritual thing spute thou no mare.
Als thou art Quene in thi quert,
Hold thes wordes in hert.
Thou shal leve but a stert;
Hethen shal thou fare."

"How shal we fare," quod the freke, "that fonden to fight,
And thus defoulen the folke on fele kinges londes,
And riches over reymes withouten eny right,
Wynnen worshipp in werre thorgh wightnesse of hondes?"
"Your King is to covetous, I warne the sir knight.
May no man stry him with strenght while his whele stondes.
Whan he is in his magesté, moost in his might,
He shal light ful lowe on the sesondes.
And this chivalrous Kinge chef shall a chaunce:
Falsely Fortune in fight,

That wonderfull wheelwryght,
Shall make lordes to light -
Take witnesse by Fraunce.

"Fraunce haf ye frely with your fight wonnen;
Freol and his folke, fey ar they leved.
Bretayne and Burgoyne al to you bowen,
And al the Dussiperes of Fraunce with your dyn deved.
Gyan may grete the werre was bigonen;
There ar no lordes on lyve in that londe leved.
Yet shal the riche Romans with you be aurronen,
And with the Rounde Table the rentes be reved;
Then shal a Tyber untrue tymber you tene.
Gete the, Sir Gawayn:
Turne the to Tuskayn.
For ye shul lese Bretayn
With a knight kene.

"This knight shal kenely croyse the crowne,
And at Carlele shal that comly be crowned as king.
That sege shal be sesede at a sesone
That myche baret and bale to Bretayn shal bring.
Hit shal in Tuskan be tolde of the treson,
And ye shullen turne ayen for the tydynge.
Ther shal the Rounde Table lese the renoune:
Beside Ramsey ful rad at a riding
In Dorsetshire shal dy the doughtest of alle.
Gete the, Sir Gawayn,
The boldest of Bretayne;
In a slake thou shal be slayne,
Sich ferlyes shull falle.

"Suche ferlies shull fal, withoute eny fable,
Uppon Cornewayle coost with a knight kene.
Sir Arthur the honest, avenant and able,
He shal be wounded, iwys - wothely, I wene.
And al the rial rowte of the Rounde Table,
Thei shullen dye on a day, the doughty bydene,
Suppriset with a suget: he beris hit in sable,
With a sauter engreled of silver full shene.
He beris hit of sable, sothely to say;
In riche Arthures halle,
The barne playes at the balle
That outray shall you alle,
Delfully that day.

"Have gode day, Gaynour, and Gawayn the gode;
I have no lenger tome tidinges to telle.
I mot walke on my wey thorgh this wilde wode
In my wonyngstid in wo for to welle.
Fore Him that rightwisly rose and rest on the Rode,
Thenke on the danger and the dole that I yn dwell.
Fede folke for my sake that failen the fode
And menge me with matens and Masse in melle.
Masses arn medecynes to us that bale bides;
Us thenke a Masse as swete
As eny spice that ever ye yete."
With a grisly grete
The goste awey glides.

With a grisly grete the goost awey glides
And goes with gronyng sore thorgh the greves grene.

The wyndes, the weders, the welken unhides -
Then unclosed the cloudes, the son con shene.
The King his bugle has blowen and on the bent bides;
His fare folke in the frith, thei flokken bydene,
And al the riall route to the Quene rides;
She sayes hem the selcouthes that thei hadde ther seen.
The wise of the weder, forwondred they were.
Prince proudest in palle,
Dame Gaynour and alle,
Went to Rondoles Halle
To the suppere.

The King to souper is set, served in sale,
Under a siller of silke dayntly dight
With al worshipp and wele, innewith the walle,
Briddes brauden and brad in bankers bright.
There come in a soteler with a symballe,
A lady lufsom of lote ledand a knight;
Ho raykes up in a res bifor the Rialle
And halsed Sir Arthur hendly on hight.
Ho said to the Soverayne, wlonkest in wede,
"Mon makeles of might,
Here commes an errant knight.
Do him reson and right
For thi manhede."

The mon in his mantell sittes at his mete
In pal pured to pay, prodly pight,
Trofelyte and traverste with trewloves in trete;
The tasses were of topas that wer thereto tight.
He gliffed up with his eighen that grey wer and grete,

With his beveren berde, on that burde bright.
He was the soveraynest of al sitting in sete
That ever segge had sen with his eye sight.
King crowned in kith carpes hir tille:
"Welcom, worthely wight -
He shal have reson and right!
Whethen is the comli knight,
If hit be thi wille?"

Ho was the worthiest wight that eny wy welde wolde;
Here gide was glorious and gay, of a gresse grene.
Here belle was of blunket, with birdes ful bolde,
Brauded with brende gold, and bokeled ful bene.
Here fax in fyne perré was fretted in folde,
Contrefelet and kelle coloured full clene,
With a crowne craftly al of clene golde.
Here kercheves were curiouse with many proude prene,
Her perré was praysed with prise men of might:
Bright birdes and bolde
Had ynoghe to beholde
Of that frely to folde,
And on the hende knight.

The knight in his colours was armed ful clene,
With his comly crest clere to beholde,
His brené and his basnet burneshed ful bene,
With a bordur abought al of brende golde.
His mayles were mylke white, enclawet ful clene;
His horse trapped of that ilke, as true men me tolde;
His shelde on his shulder of silver so shene,
With bere hedes of blake browed ful bolde;

His horse in fyne sandel was trapped to the hele.

And, in his cheveron biforne,

Stode as an unicorne,

Als sharp as a thorne,

An anlas of stele.

In stele he was stuffed, that stourne uppon stede,

Al of sternes of golde, that stanseld was one straye;

His gloves, his gamesons glowed as a glede

With graynes of rebé that graithed ben gay.

And his schene schynbaudes, that sharp wer to shrede,

His poleinus with pelydodis were poudred to pay.

With a launce on loft that lovely con lede;

A freke on a freson him folowed, in fay.

The freson was afered for drede of that fare,

For he was selden wonte to se

The tablet fluré:

Siche gamen ne gle

Sagh he never are.

Arthur asked on hight, herand him alle:

"What woldes thou, wee, if hit be thi wille?

Tel me what thou seches and whether thou shalle,

And whi thou, sturne on thi stede, stondes so stille?"

He wayved up his viser fro his ventalle;

With a knightly contenaunce, he carpes him tille:

"Whether thou be cayser or king, her I the becalle

Fore to finde me a freke to fight with my fille.

Fighting to fraist I fonded fro home."

Then seid the King uppon hight,

"If thou be curteys knight,

Late and lenge al nyght,
And tel me thi nome."

"Mi name is Sir Galaron, withouten eny gile,
The grettest of Galwey of greves and gyllis,
Of Connok, of Conyngham, and also Kyle,
Of Lomond, of Losex, of Loyan hilles.
Thou has wonen hem in werre with a wrange wile
And geven hem to Sir Gawayn - that my hert grylles.
But he shal wring his honde and warry the wyle,
Er he weld hem, ywys, agayn myn unwylles.
Bi al the welth of the worlde, he shal hem never welde,
While I the hede may bere,
But if he wyn hem in were,
With a shelde and a spere,
On a faire felde.

"I wol fight on a felde - thereto I make feith -
With eny freke uppon folde that frely is borne.
To lese suche a lordshipp me wolde thenke laith,
And iche lede opon lyve wold lagh me to scorne."
"We ar in the wode went to walke on oure waith,
To hunte at the hertes with hounde and with horne.
We ar in oure gamen; we have no gome graithe,
But yet thou shalt be mached be mydday tomorne.
Forthi I rede the, thenke rest al night."
Gawayn, grathest of all,
Ledes him oute of the hall
Into a pavilion of pall
That prodly was pight.

Pight was it prodly with purpour and palle,
Birdes brauden above, in brend gold bright.
Inwith was a chapell, a chambour, a halle,
A chymné with charcole to chaufe the knight.
His stede was stabled and led to the stalle;
Hay hertly he had in haches on hight.
Sithen thei braide up a borde, and clothes thei calle,
Sanapes and salers, semly to sight,
Torches and brochetes and stondardes bitwene.
Thus thei served that knight
And his worthely wight,
With rich dayntes dight
In silver so shene.

In silver so semely thei served of the best,
With vernage in veres and cuppes ful clene.
And thus Sir Gawayn the good glades hour gest,
With riche dayntees endored in disshes bydene.
Whan the riall renke was gone to his rest,
The King to counsaile has called his knightes so kene.
"Loke nowe, lordes, oure lose be not lost.
Ho shal encontre with the knight? Kestes you bitwene."
Then seid Gawayn the goode, "Shal hit not greve.
Here my honde I you hight,
I woll fight with the knight
In defence of my right,
Lorde, by your leve."

"I leve wel," quod the King. "Thi lates ar light,
But I nolde for no lordeshipp se thi life lorne."
"Let go!" quod Sir Gawayn. "God stond with the right!

If he skape skathlesse, hit were a foule skorne."
In the daying of the day, the doughti were dight,
And herden matens and Masse erly on morne.
By that on Plumton Land a palais was pight,
Were never freke opon folde had foughten biforne.
Thei setten listes bylyve on the logh lande.
Thre soppes demayn
Thei brought to Sir Gawayn
For to confort his brayn,
The King gared commaunde.

The King commaunded kindeli the Erlis son of Kent:
"Curtaysly in this case, take kepe to the knight."
With riche dayntees or day he dyned in his tente;
After buskes him in a brené that burneshed was bright.
Sithen to Waynour wisly he went;
He laft in here warde his worthly wight.
After aither in high hour horses thei hent,
And at the listes on the lande lordely done light
Alle bot thes two burnes, baldest of blode.
The Kinges chaier is set
Abowve on a chacelet;
Many galiard gret
For Gawayn the gode.

Gawayn and Galerone gurden her stedes;
Al in gleterand golde, gay was here gere.
The lordes bylyve hom to list ledes,
With many serjant of mace, as was the manere.
The burnes broched the blonkes that the side bledis;
Ayther freke opon folde has fastned his spere.

Shaftes in shide wode thei shindre in shedes,
So jolilé thes gentil justed on were!
Shaftes thei shindre in sheldes so shene,
And sithen, with brondes bright,
Riche mayles thei right.
There encontres the knight
With Gawayn on grene.

Gawayn was gaily grathed in grene,
With his griffons of golde engreled full gay,
Trifeled with tranes and trueloves bitwene;
On a startand stede he strikes on stray.
That other in his turnaying, he talkes in tene:
"Whi drawes thou the on dregh and makes siche deray?"
He swapped him yn at the swyre with a swerde kene;
That greved Sir Gawayn to his dethday.
The dyntes of that doughty were doutwis bydene;
Fifté mayles and mo
The swerde swapt in two,
The canelbone also,
And clef his shelde shene.

He clef thorgh the cantell that covered the knight,
Thorgh the shinand shelde a shaftmon and mare.
And then the lathely lord lowe uppon hight,
And Gawayn greches therwith and gremed ful sare:
"I shal rewarde the thi route, if I con rede right."
He folowed in on the freke with a fressh fare;
Thorgh blason and brené, that burneshed wer bright,
With a burlich bronde thorgh him he bare.
The bronde was blody that burneshed was bright.

Then gloppened that gay -
Hit was no ferly, in fay.
The sturne strikes on stray
In stiropes stright.

Streyte in his steroppes, stoutely he strikes,
And waynes at Sir Wawayn als he were wode.
Then his lemman on lowde skirles and skrikes,
When that burly burne blenket on blode.
Lordes and ladies of that laike likes
And thonked God of his grace for Gawayn the gode.
With a swap of a swerde, that swithely him swykes;
He stroke of the stede hede streite there he stode.
The faire fole fondred and fel, bi the Rode.
Gawayn gloppened in hert;
He was swithely smert.
Oute of sterops he stert
Fro Grissell the goode.

"Grissell," quod Gawayn, "gon is, God wote!
He was the burlokest blonke that ever bote brede.
By Him that in Bedeleem was borne ever to ben our bote,
I shall venge the today, if I con right rede."
"Go fecche me my freson, fairest on fote;
He may stonde the in stoure in as mekle stede."
"No more for the faire fole then for a risshrote.
But for doel of the dombe best that thus shuld be dede,
I mourne for no montur, for I may gete mare."
Als he stode by his stede,
That was so goode at nede,
Ner Gawayn wax wede,

So wepputte he sare.

Thus wepus for wo Wowayn the wight,
And wenys him to quyte, that wonded is sare.
That other drogh him on dreght for drede of the knight
And boldely broched his blonk on the bent bare.
"Thus may thou dryve forthe the day to the derk night!"
The son was passed by that mydday and mare.
Within the listes the lede lordly done light;
Touard the burne with his bronde he busked him yare.
To bataile they bowe with brondes so bright.
Shene sheldes wer shred,
Bright brenés bybled;
Many doughti were adred,
So fersely thei fight.

Thus thei feght on fote on that fair felde
As fressh as a lyon that fautes the fille.
Wilelé thes wight men thair wepenes they welde;
Wyte ye wele, Sir Gawayn wantis no will.
He brouched him yn with his bronde under the brode shelde
Thorgh the waast of the body and wonded him ille.
The swerd stent for no stuf - hit was so wel steled.
That other startis on bak and stondis stonstille.
Though he were stonayed that stonde, he strikes ful sare -
He gurdes to Sir Gawayn
Thorgh ventaile and pesayn;
He wanted noght to be slayn
The brede of an hare.

Hardely then thes hathelese on helmes they hewe.

Thei beten downe beriles and bourdures bright;
Shildes on shildres that shene were to shewe,
Fretted were in fyne golde, thei failen in fight.
Stones of iral thay strenkel and strewe;
Stithe stapeles of stele they strike done stright.
Burnes bannen the tyme the bargan was brewe,
The doughti with dyntes so delfully were dight.
The dyntis of tho doghty were doutous bydene.
Bothe Sir Lete and Sir Lake
Miche mornyng thei make.
Gaynor gret for her sake
With her grey eyen.

Thus gretis Gaynour with bothe her grey yene
For gref of Sir Gawayn, grisly was wound.
The knight of corage was cruel and kene,
And, with a stele bronde, that sturne oft stound;
Al the cost of the knyght he carf downe clene.
Thorgh the riche mailes that ronke were and rounde
With a teneful touche he taght him in tene,
He gurdes Sir Galeron groveling on gronde.
Grisly on gronde, he groned on grene.
Als wounded as he was,
Sone unredely he ras
And folowed fast on his tras
With a swerde kene.

Kenely that cruel kevered on hight,
And with a cast of the carhonde in cantil he strikes,
And waynes at Sir Wawyn, that worthely wight.
But him lymped the worse, and that me wel likes.

He atteled with a slenk haf slayn him in slight;
The swerd swapped on his swange and on the mayle slikes,
And Gawayn bi the coler keppes the knight.
Then his lemman on loft skrilles and skrikes -
Ho gretes on Gaynour with gronyng grylle:
"Lady makeles of might,
Haf mercy on yondre knight
That is so delfull dight,
If hit be thi wille."

Than wilfully Dame Waynour to the King went;
Ho caught of her coronall and kneled him tille:
"As thou art Roye roial, richest of rent,
And I thi wife wedded at thi owne wille -
Thes burnes in the bataile so blede on the bent,
They arn wery, iwis, and wonded full ille.
Thorgh her shene sheldes, her shuldres ar shent;
The grones of Sir Gawayn dos my hert grille.
The grones of Sir Gawayne greven me sare.
Wodest thou leve, Lorde,
Make thes knightes accorde,
Hit were a grete conforde
For all that here ware."

Then spak Sir Galeron to Gawayn the good:
"I wende never wee in this world had ben half so wight.
Here I make the releyse, renke, by the Rode,
And, byfore thiese ryalle, resynge the my ryghte;
And sithen make the monraden with a mylde mode
As man of medlert makeles of might."
He talkes touard the King on hie ther he stode,

And bede that burly his bronde that burneshed was bright:
"Of rentes and richesse I make the releyse."
Downe kneled the knight
And carped wordes on hight;
The King stode upright
And commaunded pes.

The King commaunded pes and cried on hight,
And Gawayn was goodly and laft for his sake.
Then lordes to listes they lopen ful light -
Sir Ewayn Fiz Uryayn and Arrak Fiz Lake,
Marrake and Moylard, that most wer of might -
Bothe thes travayled men they truly up take.
Unneth might tho sturne stonde upright -
What, for buffetes and blode, her blees wex blak;
Her blees were brosed, for beting of brondes.
Withouten more lettyng,
Dight was here saghtlyng;
Bifore the comly King,
Thei held up her hondes.

"Here I gif Sir Gawayn, with gerson and golde,
Al the Glamergan londe with greves so grene,
The worship of Wales at wil and at wolde,
With Criffones Castelles curnelled ful clene;
Eke Ulstur Halle to hafe and to holde,
Wayford and Waterforde, wallede I wene;
Two baronrees in Bretayne with burghes so bolde,
That arn batailed abought and bigged ful bene.
I shal doue the a duke and dubbe the with honde,
Withthi thou saghtil with the knight

That is so hardi and wight,
And relese him his right,
And graunte him his londe."

"Here I gif Sir Galeron," quod Gawayn, "withouten any gile,
Al the londes and the lithes fro Lauer to Layre,
Connoke and Carlele, Conyngham and Kile;
Yet, if he of chevalry chalange ham for aire,
The Lother, the Lemmok, the Loynak, the Lile,
With frethis and forestes and fosses so faire.
Withthi under our lordeship thou lenge here a while,
And to the Round Table make thy repaire,
I shal refeff the in felde in forestes so fair."
Bothe the King and the Quene
And al the doughti bydene,
Thorgh the greves so grene,
To Carlele thei cair.

The King to Carlele is comen with knightes so kene,
And al the Rounde Table on rial aray.
The wees that weren wounded so wothely, I wene,
Surgenes sone saned, sothely to say;
Bothe confortes the knightes, the King and the Quene.
Thei were dubbed dukes both on a day.
There he wedded his wife, wlonkest I wene,
With giftes and garsons, Sir Galeron the gay;
Thus that hathel in high withholdes that hende.
Whan he was saned sonde,
Thei made Sir Galeron that stonde
A knight of the Table Ronde
To his lyves ende.

Waynour gared wisely write into the west
To al the religious to rede and to singe;
Prestes with procession to pray were prest,
With a mylion of Masses to make the mynnynge.
Bokelered men, bisshops the best,
Thorgh al Bretayne belles the burde gared rynge.
This ferely bifelle in Ingulwud Forest,
Under a holte so hore at a huntyng -
Suche a huntyng in holtis is noght to be hide.
Thus to forest they fore,
Thes sterne knightes in store.
In the tyme of Arthore
This anter betide.
Thou arte so semely to see,
   And thou were wele dighte!"

He saide, "And thou were wele dighte,
Thou were lyke to a knyghte
That I lovede with all my myghte
   Whills he was one lyve.
So wele wroghte he my will
In all manere of skill,
I gaffe my syster hym till,
   For to be his wyfe.
He es moste in my mane:
Fiftene yere es it gane,
Sen a theffe hade hym slane
   Abowte a littill stryffe!
Sythen hafe I ever bene his fo,
For to wayte hym with wo.

Bot I myghte hym never slo,
  His craftes are so ryfe."

He sayse, "His craftes are so ryfe,
Ther is no man apon lyfe,
With swerde, spere, ne with knyfe
  May stroye hym allan,
Bot if it were Sir Percyvell son.
Whoso wiste where he ware done!
The bokes says that he mon
  Venge his fader bane."
The childe thoghte he longe bade
That he ne ware a knyghte made,
For he wiste never that he hade
  A fader to be slayne;
The lesse was his menynge.
He saide sone to the Kynge,
"Sir, late be thi jangleynge!
  Of this kepe I nane."

He sais, "I kepe not to stande
With thi jangleyns to lange.
Make me knyghte with thi hande,
  If it sall be done!"
Than the Kyng hym hendly highte
That he schold dub hym to knyghte,
With thi that he wolde doun lighte
  And ete with hym at none.
The Kyng biholdes the vesage free,
And ever more trowed hee
That the childe scholde bee

Sir Percyvell son:
It ran in the Kynges mode,
His syster Acheflour the gude -
How scho went into the wodde
  With hym for to wonn.

The childe hadde wonnede in the wodde;
He knewe nother evyll ne gude;
The Kynge hymselfe understode
  He was a wilde man.
So faire he spakke hym withall,
He lyghtes doun in the haulle,
Bonde his mere amonge tham alle
  And to the borde wann.
Bot are he myghte bygynn
To the mete for to wynn,
So commes the Rede Knyghte in
  Emanges tham righte than,
Prekande one a rede stede;
Blode-rede was his wede.
He made tham gammen full gnede,
  With craftes that he can.

With his craftes gan he calle,
And callede tham recrayhandes all,
Kynge, knyghtes inwith walle,
  At the bordes ther thay bade.
Full felly the coupe he fett,
Bifore the Kynge that was sett.
Ther was no man that durste hym lett,
  Thofe that he were fadde.

The couppe was filled full of wyne;
He dranke of that that was therinn.
All of rede golde fyne
  Was the couppe made.
He tuke it up in his hande,
The coupe that he there fande,
And lefte tham all sittande,
  And fro tham he rade.

Now from tham he rade,
Als he says that this made.
The sorowe that the Kynge hade
  Mighte no tonge tell.
"A! dere God," said the Kyng than,
"That all this wyde werlde wan,
Whethir I sall ever hafe that man
  May make yone fende duelle?
Fyve yeres hase he thus gane,
And my coupes fro me tane,
And my gude knyghte slayne,
  Men calde Sir Percyvell;
Sythen taken hase he three,
And ay awaye will he bee,
Or I may harnayse me
  In felde hym to felle."

"Petir!" quod Percyvell the yonge,
"Hym than will I down dynge
And the coupe agayne brynge,
  And thou will make me knyghte."

"Als I am trewe kyng," said he,
"A knyghte sall I make the,
Forthi thou will brynge mee
   The coupe of golde bryghte."
Up ryses Sir Arthoure,
Went to a chamboure
To feche doun armoure,
   The childe in to dyghte;
Bot are it was doun caste,
Ere was Percyvell paste,
And on his way folowed faste,
   That he solde with fyghte.

With his foo for to fighte,
None othergates was he dighte,
Bot in thre gayt-skynnes righte,
   A fole als he ware.

He cryed, "How, man on thi mere!
Bryng agayne the Kynges gere,
Or with my dart I sall the fere
   And make the unfere!"
And after the Rede Knyghte he rade,
Baldely, withowtten bade:
Sayd, "A knyght I sall be made
   For som of thi gere."
He sware by mekill Goddes payne,
"Bot if thou brynge the coupe agayne,
With my dart thou sall be slayne
   And slongen of thi mere."

The kynghte byhaldes hym in throo,
Calde hym fole that was hys foo,
For he named hym soo -
   The stede that hym bere.

And for to see hym with syghte,
He putt his umbrere on highte,
To byhalde how he was dyghte,
   That so till hym spake.
He sayde, "Come I to the, appert fole;
I sall caste the in the pole,
For all the heghe days of Yole,
   Als ane olde sakke."
Than sayd Percyvell the free,
"Be I fole, or whatte I bee,
Now sone of that sall wee see
   Whose browes schall blakke."
Of schottyng was the childe slee:
At the knyghte lete he flee,
Smote hym in at the eghe
   And oute at the nakke.

For the dynt that he tuke,
Oute of sadill he schoke,
Whoso the sothe will luke,
   And ther was he slayne.
He falles down one the hill;
His stede rynnes whare he will.
Than saide Percyvell hym till,
   "Thou art a lethir swayne."
Then saide the childe in that tyde,

"And thou woldeste me here byde,
After thi mere scholde I ryde
  And brynge hir agayne;
Then myghte we bothe with myghte
Menskfully togedir fyghte,
Ayther of us, as he were a knyghte,
  Till tyme the tone ware slayne."

Now es the Rede Knyghte slayne,
Lefte dede in the playne.
The childe gon his mere mayne
  After the stede.
The stede was swifter than the mere,
For he hade no thynge to bere
Bot his sadill and his gere,
  Fro hym thofe he yede.
The mere was bagged with fole;
And hirselfe a grete bole;
For to rynne scho myghte not thole,
  Ne folowe hym no spede.
The childe saw that it was soo,
And till his fete he gan hym too;
The gates that he scholde goo
  Made he full gnede.

The gates made he full gnede
In the waye ther he yede;
With strenght tuke he the stede
  And broghte to the knyghte.
"Me thynke," he sayde, "thou arte fele
That thou ne will away stele;

Now I houppe that thou will dele
  Strokes appon hyghte.
I hafe broghte to the thi mere
And mekill of thyn other gere;
Lepe on hir, as thou was ere,
  And thou will more fighte!"
The knyghte lay still in the stede:
What sulde he say, when he was dede?
The childe couthe no better rede,
  Bot down gun he lyghte.

Now es Percyvell lyghte
To unspoyle the Rede Knyghte,
Bot he ne couthe never fynd righte
  The lacynge of his wede.
He was armede so wele
In gude iryn and in stele,
He couthe no gett of a dele,
  For nonkyns nede.
He sayd, "My moder bad me,
When my dart solde broken be,
Owte of the iren bren the tree:
  Now es me fyre gnede."
Now he getis hym flynt,
His fyre-iren he hent,
And then, withowtten any stynt,
  He kyndilt a glede.

Now he kyndils a glede,
Amonge the buskes he yede
And gedirs, full gude spede,

   Wodde, a fyre to make.
A grete fyre made he than,
The Rede Knyghte in to bren,
For he ne couthe nott ken
   His gere off to take.
Be than was Sir Gawayne dyght,
Folowede after the fyghte
Betwene hym and the Rede Knyghte,
   For the childes sake.
He fande the Rede Knyght lyggand,
Slayne of Percyvell hande,
Besyde a fyre brynnande
   Off byrke and of akke.

Ther brent of birke and of ake
Gret brandes and blake.
"What wylt thou with this fyre make?"
   Sayd Gawayne hym till.
"Petir!" quod Percyvell then,
"And I myghte hym thus ken,
Out of his iren I wolde hym bren
   Righte here on this hill."
Bot then sayd Sir Gawayne,
"The Rede Knyghte for thou has slayne,
I sall unarme hym agayne,
   And thou will holde the still."
Than Sir Gawayn doun lyghte,
Unlacede the Rede Knyghte;
The childe in his armour dight
   At his awnn will.

When he was dighte in his atire,
He tase the knyghte bi the swire,
Keste hym reghte in the fyre,
    The brandes to balde.
Bot then said Percyvell on bost,
"Ly still therin now and roste!
I kepe nothynge of thi coste,
    Ne noghte of thi spalde!"
The knyghte lygges ther on brede;
The childe es dighte in his wede,
And lepe up apon his stede,
    Als hymselfe wolde.
He luked doun to his fete,
Saw his gere faire and mete:
"For a knyghte I may be lete
    And myghte be calde."

Then sayd Sir Gawayn hym till,
"Goo we faste fro this hill!
Thou hase done what thou will;
    It neghes nere nyghte."
"What! trowes thou," quod Percyvell the yonge,
"That I will agayn brynge
Untill Arthoure the Kynge
    The golde that es bryghte?
Nay, so mote I thryfe or thee,
I am als grete a lorde als he;
To-day ne schall he make me
    None other gates knyghte.
Take the coupe in thy hande

And mak thiselfe the presande,
For I will forthire into the lande,
  Are I doun lyghte."

Nowther wolde he doun lyghte,
Ne he wolde wende with the knyght,
Bot rydes forthe all the nyghte,
  So prowde was he than.
Till on the morne at forthe dayes,
He mett a wyche, as men says.
His horse and his harnays
  Couthe scho wele ken.
Scho wende that it hade bene
The Rede Knyghte that scho hade sene,
Was wonnt in those armes to bene,
  To gerre the stede rynne.
In haste scho come hym agayne,
Sayde, "It is not to layne,
Men tolde me that thou was slayne
  With Arthours men.

Ther come one of my men,
Till yonder hill he gan me kenne,
There thou sees the fyre brene,
  And sayde that thou was thare."
Ever satt Percyvell stone-still,
And spakke no thynge hir till
Till scho hade sayde all hir will,
  And spakke lesse ne mare.
"At yondere hill hafe I bene:
Nothynge hafe I there sene

Bot gayte-skynnes, I wene.
  Siche ill-farande fare!"
"Mi sone, and thou ware thare slayne
And thyn armes of drawen,
I couthe hele the agayne
  Als wele als thou was are."

Than wist Percyvell by thatt,
It servede hym of somwhatt,
The wylde fyre that he gatt
  When the knyghte was slayne;
And righte so wolde he, thare
That the olde wiche ware.
Oppon his spere he hir bare
  To the fyre agayne;
In ill wrethe and in grete,
He keste the wiche in the hete;
He sayde, "Ly still and swete
  Bi thi son, that lyther swayne!"
Thus he leves thaym twoo,
And on his gates gan he goo:
Siche dedis to do moo
  Was the childe fayne.

Als he come by a wodd-syde,
He sawe ten men ryde;
He said, "For oughte that may betyde,
  To tham will I me."
When those ten saw hym thare,
Thay wende the Rede Knyghte it ware,
That wolde tham all forfare,

And faste gan thay flee;
For he was sogates cledde,
Alle belyffe fro hym thay fledde;
And ever the faster that thay spedde,
  The swiftlyere sewed hee,
Till he was warre of a knyghte,
And of the menevaire he had syght;
He put up his umbrere on hight,
  And said, "Sir, God luke thee!"

The childe sayde, "God luke the!"
The knyght said, "Now wele the be!
A, lorde Godd, now wele es mee
  That ever was I made!"
For by the vesage hym thoghte
The Rede Knyghte was it noghte,
That hade them all bysoughte;
  And baldely he bade.
It semede wele bi the syghte
That he had slayne the Rede Knyght:
In his armes was he dighte,
  And on his stede rade.
"Son," sayde the knyghte tho,
And thankede the childe full thro,
"Thou hase slayne the moste foo
  That ever yitt I hade."

Then sayde Percyvell the free,
"Wherefore fledde yee
Lange are, when ye sawe mee

Come rydande yow by?"
Bot than spake the olde knyghte,
That was paste out of myghte
With any man for to fyghte:
   He ansuerde in hy;
He sayde, "Theis children nyne,
All are thay sonnes myne.
For ferde or I solde tham tyne,
   Therfore fledd I.
We wende wele that it had bene
The Rede Knyghte that we hade sene;
He walde hafe slayne us bydene,
   Withowtten mercy.

Withowtten any mercy
He wolde hafe slayne us in hy;
To my sonnes he hade envy
   Moste of any men.
Fiftene yeres es it gane
Syn he my brodire hade slane;
Now hadde the theefe undirtane
   To sla us all then:
He was ferde lesse my sonnes sold hym slo
When thay ware eldare and moo,
And that thay solde take hym for thaire foo
   Where thay myghte hym ken;
Hade I bene in the stede
Ther he was done to the dede,
I solde never hafe etyn brede
   Are I hade sene hym bren."

"Petir!" quod Percyvell, "he es brende!
I haffe spedde better than I wend
Ever at the laste ende."
   The blythere wexe the knyghte;
By his haulle thaire gates felle,
And yerne he prayed Percyvell
That he solde ther with hym duelle
   And be ther all that nyghte.
Full wele he couthe a geste calle.
He broghte the childe into the haulle;
So faire he spake hym withalle
   That he es doun lyghte;
His stede es in stable sett
And hymselfe to the haulle fett,
And than, withowtten any lett,
   To the mette thay tham dighte.

Mete and drynke was ther dighte,
And men to serve tham full ryghte;
The childe that come with the knyghte,
   Enoghe ther he fande.
At the mete as thay beste satte,
Come the portere fro the gate,
Saide a man was theratte
   Of the Maydenlande;
Saide, "Sir, he prayes the
Off mete and drynke, for charyté;
For a messagere es he
   And may nott lange stande."
The knyght badde late hym inn,
"For," he sayde, "it es no synn,

The man that may the mete wynn
To gyffe the travellande."

Now the travellande man
The portere lete in than;
He haylsede the knyghte as he can,
    Als he satt on dese.
The knyghte askede hym thare
Whase man that he ware,
And how ferre that he walde so fare,
    Withowtten any lese.
He saide, "I come fro the Lady Lufamour,
That sendes me to Kyng Arthoure,
And prayes hym, for his honoure,
    Hir sorowes for to sesse.
Up resyn es a Sowdane:
Alle hir landes hase he tane;
So byseges he that woman
    That scho may hafe no pese."

He sayse that scho may have no pese,
The lady, for hir fayrenes,
And for hir mekill reches.
    "He wirkes hir full woo;
He dose hir sorow all hir sythe,
And all he slaes doun rythe;
He wolde have hir to wyfe,
    And scho will noghte soo.
Now hase that ilke Sowdane
Hir fadir and hir eme slane,
And hir brethir ilkane,

And is hir moste foo.
So nere he hase hir now soughte
That till a castelle es scho broghte,
And fro the walles will he noghte,
   Ere that he may hir too.

The Sowdane sayse he will hir ta;
The lady will hirselfe sla
Are he, that es hir maste fa,
   Solde wedde hir to wyfe.
Now es the Sowdan so wyghte,
Alle he slaes doun ryghte:
Ther may no man with hym fyghte,
   Bot he were kempe ryfe."
Than sayde Percyvell, "I the praye,
That thou wolde teche me the waye
Thedir, als the gates laye,
   Withowtten any stryfe;
Mighte I mete with that Sowdan
That so dose to that woman,
Alsone he solde be slane,
   And I myghte hafe the lyfe!"

The messangere prayed hym mare
That he wolde duell still thare:
"For I will to the Kynge fare,
   Myne erandes for to say.
For then mekill sorowe me betyde,
And I lenger here habyde,
Bot ryghte now will I ryde,

Als so faste als I may."
The knyghte herde hym say so;
Yerne he prayes hym to too
His nyne sonnes, with hym to goo.
    He nykkes hym with nay.
Bot so faire spekes he
That he takes of tham three,
In his felawchipe to be -
    The blythere were thay.

Thay ware blythe of ther bade,
Busked tham and forthe rade;
Mekill myrthes thay made:
    Bot lyttill it amende.
He was paste bot a while -
The montenance of a myle -
He was bythoghte of a gyle
    Wele werse than thay wende.
Thofe thay ware of thaire fare fayne,
Forthwarde was thaire cheftayne;
Ever he sende on agayne
    At ilke a myle ende,
Untill thay ware alle gane;
Than he rydes hym allane
Als he ware sprongen of a stane,
    Thare na man hym kende,

For he walde none sold hym ken.
Forthe rydes he then,
Amanges uncouthe men
    His maystres to make.

Now hase Percyvell in throo
Spoken with his emes twoo,
Bot never one of thoo
   Took his knawlage.
Now in his way es he sett
That may hym lede, withowtten lett,
Thare he and the Sowdan sall mete,
   His browes to blake.
Late we Percyvell the yynge
Fare in Goddes blyssynge,
And untill Arthoure the Kynge
   Will we agayne take.

The gates agayne we will tane:
The Kyng to care-bedd es gane;
For mournynge es his maste mane.
   He syghes full sore.
His wo es wansome to wreke,
His hert es bownn for to breke,
For he wend never to speke
   With Percyvell no more.
Als he was layde for to ly,
Come the messangere on hy
With lettres fro the lady,
   And schewes tham righte thare.
Afote myghte the Kyng noght stande,
Bot rede tham thare lyggande,
And sayde, "Of thyne erande
   Thou hase thyn answare."

He sayde, "Thou wote thyne ansuare:

The mane that es seke and sare,
He may full ill ferre fare
   In felde for to fyghte."
The messangere made his mone:
Saide, "Wo worthe wikkede wone!
Why ne hade I tournede and gone
   Agayne with the knyghte?"
"What knyghte es that," said the Kyng,
"That thou mase of thy menynge?
In my londe wot I no lordyng
   Es worthy to be a knyghte."
The messangere ansuerd agayne,
"Wete ye, his name es for to layne,
The whethir I wolde hafe weten fayne
   What the childe highte.

Thus mekill gatt I of that knyght:
His dame sonne, he said, he hight.
One what maner that he was dight
   Now I sall yow telle:
He was wighte and worthly,
His body bolde and borely,
His armour bryghte and blody -
   Hade bene late in batell;
Blode-rede was his stede,
His akton, and his other wede;
His cote of the same hede
   That till a knyghte felle."
Than comanded the Kyng
Horse and armes for to brynge:
"If I kan trow thi talkynge,

That ilke was Percyvell."

For the luffe of Percyvell,
To horse and armes thay felle;
Thay wolde no lengare ther duelle:
　To fare ware thay fayne.
Faste forthe gan thay fare;
Thay were aferde full sare,
Ere thay come whare he ware,
　The childe wolde be slayne.
The Kyng tase with hym knyghtis thre:
The ferthe wolde hymselfe be;
Now so faste rydes hee,
　May folowe hym no swayne.
The Kyng es now in his waye;
Lete hym come when he maye!
And I will forthir in my playe
　To Percyvell agayne.

Go we to Percyvell agayne.
The childe paste oute on the playne,
Over more and mountayne,
　To the Maydenlande;
Till agayne the even-tyde,
Bolde bodys sawe he byde,
Pavelouns mekill and unryde
　Aboute a cyté stonde.
On huntyng was the Sowdane;
He lefte men many ane,
Twenty score that wele kan:

Be the gates yemande -
Elleven score one the nyghte,
And ten one the daye-lighte -
Wele armyde at alle righte,
  With wapyns in hande.

With thaire wapyns in thaire hande,
There will thay fight ther thay stande,
Sittande and lyggande,
  Elleven score of men.
In he rydes one a rase,
Or that he wiste where he was,
Into the thikkeste of the prese
  Amanges tham thanne.
And up stirt one that was bolde,
Bygane his brydill to holde,
And askede whedire that he wolde
  Make his horse to rynne.
He said, "I ame hedir come
For to see a Sowdane;
In faythe, righte sone he sall be slane,
  And I myghte hym ken.

If I hym oghte ken may,
To-morne, when it es lighte daye
Than sall we togedir playe
  With wapyns unryde."
They herde that he had undirtane
For to sle thaire Sowdane.
Thay felle aboute hym, everilkane,
  To make that bolde habyde.

The childe sawe that he was fade,
The body that his bridill hade:
Even over hym he rade,
  In gate there bisyde.
He stayred about hym with his spere;
Many thurgh gane he bere:
Ther was none that myght hym dere,
  Percevell, that tyde.

Tide in townne who will telle,
Folkes undir his fete felle;
The bolde body Percevelle,
  He sped tham to spill.
Hym thoghte no spede at his spere:
Many thurgh gane he bere,
Fonde folke in the here,
  Feghtyng to fill.
Fro that it was mydnyghte
Till it was even at daye-lighte,
Were thay never so wilde ne wighte,
  He wroghte at his will.
Thus he dalt with his brande,
There was none that myght hym stande
Halfe a dynt of his hande
  That he stroke till.

Now he strykes for the nonys,
Made the Sarazenes hede-bones
Hoppe als dose hayle-stones
  Abowtte one the gres;
Thus he dalt tham on rawe

Till the daye gun dawe:
He layd thaire lyves full law,
    Als many als there was.
When he hade slayne so many men,
He was so wery by then,
I tell yow for certen,
    He roghte wele the lesse
Awther of lyfe or of dede;
To medis that he were in a stede
Thar he myghte riste hym in thede
    A stownde in sekirnes.

Now fonde he no sekirnes,
Bot under the walle ther he was,
A faire place he hym chese,
    And down there he lighte.
He laide hym doun in that tyde;
His stede stode hym besyde:
The fole was fayne for to byde -
    Was wery for the fyght
Till one the morne that it was day.
The wayte appon the walle lay:
He sawe an uggly play
    In the place dighte;
Yitt was ther more ferly:
Ther was no qwyk man left therby!
Thay called up the lady
    For to see that sighte.

Now commes the lady to that sight,

The Lady Lufamour, the brighte;
Scho clambe up to the walle on hight
    Full faste to beholde;
Hedes and helmys ther was
(I tell yow withowtten lese),
Many layde one the gresse,
    And many schelde brode.
Grete ferly thaym thoghte
Who that wondir had wroghte,
That had tham to dede broghte,
    That folke in the felde,
And wold come none innermare
For to kythe what he ware,
And wist the lady was thare,
    Thaire warysoune to yelde.

Scho wold thaire warysone yelde:
Full faste forthe thay bihelde
If thay myghte fynde in the felde
    Who hade done that dede;
Thay luked undir thair hande,
Sawe a mekill horse stande,
A blody knyghte liggande
    By a rede stede.
Then said the lady so brighte,
"Yondir ligges a knyghte
That hase bene in the fighte,
    If I kane righte rede;
Owthir es yone man slane,
Or he slepis hym allane,
Or he in batelle es tane,

For blody are his wede."

Scho says, "Blody are his wede,
And so es his riche stede;
Siche a knyght in this thede
   Saw I never nane.
What so he es, and he maye ryse,
He es large there he lyse,
And wele made in alle wyse,
   Ther als man sall be tane."
Scho calde appon hir chaymbirlayne,
Was called hende Hatlayne -
The curtasye of Wawayne
   He weldis in wane;
Scho badd hym, "Wende and see
Yif yon man on lyfe be.
Bid hym com and speke with me,
   And pray hym als thou kane."

Now to pray hym als he kane,
Undir the wallis he wane;
Warly wakend he that mane:
   The horse stode still.
Als it was tolde unto me,
He knelid down on his kne;
Hendely hailsed he that fre,
   And sone said hym till,
"My lady, lele Lufamour,
Habyddis the in hir chambour,
Prayes the, for thyn honour,
   To come, yif ye will."

So kyndly takes he that kyth
That up he rose and went hym wyth,
The man that was of myche pyth
    Hir prayer to fulfill.

Now hir prayer to fulfill,
He folowed the gentilmans will,
And so he went hir untill,
    Forthe to that lady.
Full blythe was that birde brighte
When scho sawe hym with syghte,
For scho trowed that he was wighte,
    And askede hym in hy:
At that fre gan scho frayne,
Thoghe he were lefe for to layne,
If he wiste who had tham slayne -
    Thase folkes of envy.
He sayd, "I soghte none of tho;
I come the Sowdane to slo,
And thay ne wolde noghte late me go;
    Thaire lyfes there refte I."

He sayd, "Belyfe thay solde aby."
And Lufamour, that lele lady,
Wist ful wele therby
    The childe was full wighte.
The birde was blythe of that bade
That scho siche and helpe hade;
Agayne the Sowdane was fade
    With alle for to fighte.
Faste the lady hym byhelde:

Scho thoght hym worthi to welde,
And he myghte wyn hir in felde,
  With maystry and myghte.
His stede thay in stabill set
And hymselfe to haulle was fet,
And than, withowtten any let,
  To dyne gun thay dighte.

The childe was sett on the dese,
And served with reches -
I tell yow withowtten lese -
  That gaynely was get,
In a chayere of golde
Bifore the fayrest, to byholde
The myldeste mayden one molde,
  At mete als scho satt.
Scho made hym semblande so gude,
Als thay felle to thaire fude,
The mayden mengede his mode
  With myrthes at the mete,
That for hir sake righte tha
Sone he gane undirta
The sory Sowdane to sla,
  Withowtten any lett.

He sayd, withowtten any lett,
"When the Sowdane and I bene mett,
A sadde stroke I sall one hym sett,
  His pride for to spyll."
Then said the lady so free,

"Who that may his bon be
Sall hafe this kyngdome and me,
   To welde at his will."
He ne hade dyned bot smalle
When worde come into the haulle
That many men withalle
   Were hernyste one the hill;
For tene thaire felawes were slayne,
The cité hafe thay nere tane.
The men that were within the wane
   The comon-belle gun knylle.

Now knyllyn thay the comon-belle.
Worde come to Percevell,
And he wold there no lengere duelle,
   Bot lepe fro the dese -
Siche wilde gerys hade he mo -
Sayd, "Kynsmen, now I go.
For alle yone sall I slo
   Longe are I sese!"
Scho kiste hym withowtten lett;
The helme on his hede scho sett;
To the stabill full sone he gett,
   There his stede was.
There were none with hym to fare;
For no man then wolde he spare! -
Rydis furthe, withowtten mare,
   Till he come to the prese.

When he come to the prese,
He rydes in one a rese;

The folkes, that byfore hym was,
    Thaire strenght hade thay tone;
To kepe hym than were thay ware;
Thaire dynttis deris hym no mare
Then whoso hade strekyn sare
    One a harde stone.
Were thay wighte, were thay woke,
Alle that he till stroke,
He made thaire bodies to roke:
    Was ther no better wone.
I wote, he sped hym so sone
That day, by heghe none
With all that folke hade he done:
    One lefe lefte noghte one.

When he had slayne all tho,
He loked forthir hym fro,
If he myghte fynde any mo
    With hym for to fyghte;
And als that hardy bihelde,
He sese, ferre in the felde,
Fowre knyghtis undir schelde
    Come rydand full righte.
One was Kyng Arthour,
Anothir Ewayne, the floure,
The thirde Wawayne with honoure,
    And Kay, the kene knyghte.
Percevell saide, withowtten mare,
"To yondir foure will I fare;
And if the Sowdane be thare,
    I sall holde that I highte."

Now to holde that he hase highte,
Agaynes thaym he rydis righte,
And ay lay the lady brighte
   One the walle, and byhelde
How many men that he had slane,
And sythen gane his stede mayne
Foure kempys agayne,
   Forthir in the felde.
Then was the lady full wo
When scho sawe hym go
Agaynes foure knyghtys tho,
   With schafte and with schelde.
They were so mekyl and unryde
That wele wende scho that tyde
With bale thay solde gare hym byde
   That was hir beste belde.

Thofe he were beste of hir belde,
As that lady byhelde,
He rydes forthe in the felde,
   Even tham agayne.
Then sayd Arthoure the Kyng,
"I se a bolde knyghte owt spryng;
For to seke feghtyng,
   Forthe will he frayne.
If he fare forthe to fighte
And we foure kempys agayne one knyght,
Littill menske wold to us lighte
   If he were sone slayne."
They fore forthward right faste,

And sone kevells did thay caste,
And evyr fell it to frayste
Untill Sir Wawayne.

When it felle to Sir Wawayne
To ryde Percevell agayne,
Of that fare was he fayne,
   And fro tham he rade.
Ever the nerre hym he drewe,
Wele the better he hym knewe,
Horse and hernays of hewe,
That the childe hade.
"A, dere God!" said Wawayne the fre,
"How-gates may this be?
If I sle hym, or he me,
   That never yit was fade,
And we are sisters sones two,
And aythir of us othir slo,
He that lifes will be full wo
   That ever was he made."

Now no maistrys he made,
Sir Wawayne, there als he rade,
Bot hovyde styll and habade
   His concell to ta.
"Ane unwyse man," he sayd, "am I,
That puttis myselfe to siche a foly;
Es there no man so hardy
   That ne anothir es alswa.
Thogfe Percevell hase slayne the Rede Knight,

Yitt may another be als wyghte,
And in that gere be dyghte,
   And taken alle hym fra.
If I suffire my sister sone,
And anothir in his gere be done
And gete the maystry me appon,
   That wolde do me wa;

It wolde wirke me full wa!
So mote I one erthe ga,
It ne sall noghte betyde me swa,
   If I may righte rede!
A schafte sall I one hym sett,
And I sall fonde firste to hitt;
Then sall I ken be my witt
   Who weldys that wede."
No more carpys he that tyde,
Bot son togedyr gon thay ryde-
Men that bolde were to byde,
   And styff appon stede;
Thaire horse were stallworthe and strange,
Thair scheldis were unfailande;
Thaire speris brake to thaire hande,
   Als tham byhoved nede.

Now es broken that are were hale,
And than bygane Percevale
For to tell one a tale
   That one his tonge laye.
He sayde, "Wyde-whare hafe I gane;
Siche anothir Sowdane

In faythe sawe I never nane,
  By nyghte ne by daye.
I hafe slayne, and I the ken,
Twenty score of thi men;
And of alle that I slewe then,
  Me thoghte it bot a playe
Agayne that dynt that I hafe tane;
For siche one aughte I never nane
Bot I qwyte two for ane,
  Forsothe, and I maye."

Then spake Sir Wawayne -
Certanely, is noghte to layne -
Of that fare was he fayne,
  In felde there thay fighte:
By the wordis so wylde
At the fole one the felde,
He wiste wele it was the childe,
  Percevell the wighte -
He sayse, "I ame no Sowdane,
Bot I am that ilke man
That thi body bygan
  In armours to dighte.
I giffe the prise to thi pyth.
Unkyndely talked thou me with:
My name es Wawayne in kythe,
  Whoso redys righte."

He says, "Who that will rede the aryghte,
My name es Wawayne the knyghte."
And than thay sessen of thaire fighte,

    Als gude frendes scholde.
He sayse, "Thynkes thou noghte when
That thou woldes the knyghte brene,
For thou ne couthe noghte ken
    To spoyle hym alle colde?"
Bot then was Percevell the free
Als blythe als he myghte be,
For then wiste he wele that it was he,
    By takens that he tolde.
He dide then als he gane hym lere:
Putt up hys umbrere;
And kyste togedir with gud chere
    Those beryns so bolde.

Now kissede the beryns so bolde,
Sythen talkede what thay wolde.
Be then come Arthour the bolde,
    That there was knyghte and kyng
Als his cosyns hadd done,
Thankede God also sone.
Off mekill myrthis thay mone
    At thaire metyng.
Sythen, withowtten any bade,
To the castelle thay rade
With the childe that thay hade,
    Percevell the yynge.
The portere was redy thare,
Lete the knyghtis in fare;
A blythere lady than . . .
        . . . .

"Mi grete socour at thou here sende,
Off my castell me to diffende,
Agayne the Sowdane to wende,
　That es my moste foo."
Theire stedis thay sett in the stalle.
The Kyng wendis to haulle;
His knyghtis yode hym with alle,
　Als kynde was to go.
Thaire metis was redy,
And therto went thay in hy,
The Kyng and the lady,
　And knyghtis also.

Wele welcomed scho the geste
With riche metis of the beste,
Drynkes of the derreste,
　Dighted bydene.
Thay ete and dranke what thay wolde,
Sythen talked and tolde
Off othir estres full olde,
　The Kyng and the Qwene.
At the firste bygynnyng,
Scho frayned Arthour the Kyng
Of childe Percevell the yyng,
　What life he had in bene.
Grete wondir had Lufamour
He was so styffe in stour
And couthe so littill of nurtour
　Als scho had there sene.

Scho had sene with the childe

No thyng bot werkes wylde:
Thoghte grete ferly on filde
  Of that foly fare.
Then said Arthour the Kyng
Of bold Percevell techyng,
Fro the firste bygynnyng
  Till that he come thar:
How his fadir was slayne,
And his modir to the wode gane
For to be there hir allane
  In the holtis hare,
Fully feftene yere
To play hym with the wilde dere:
Littill wonder it were
  Wilde if he ware!

When he had tolde this tale
To that semely in sale
He hade wordis at wale
  To tham ilkane.
Then said Percevell the wighte,
"Yif I be noghte yitt knyghte,
Thou sall halde that thou highte,
  For to make me ane."
Than saide the Kyng full sone,
"Ther sall other dedis be done,
And thou sall wynn thi schone
  Appon the Sowdane."
Then said Percevell the fre,
"Als sone als I the Sowdane see,
Righte so sall it sone be,

Als I hafe undirtane."

He says, "Als I hafe undirtane
For to sla the Sowdane,
So sall I wirke als I kanne,
   That dede to bygynn."
That day was ther no more dede
With those worthily in wede,
Bot buskede tham and to bedde yede,
   The more and the mynn;
Till one the morne erely
Comes the Sowdane with a cry,
Fonde all his folkes hym by
   Putt into pyn.
Sone asked he wha
That so durste his men sla,
And wete hym one lyfe gaa,
   The maystry to wynn.

Now to wynn the maystry,
To the castell gan he cry,
If any were so hardy,
   The maistry to wynn:
"A man for ane,
Thoghe he hadd all his folke slane,
Here sall he fynde Golrotherame
   To mete hym full ryghte,
Appon siche a covenande
That ye hefe up your hande;
Who that may the better stande
   And more es of myghte

To bryng that other to the dede,
Browke wele the londe on brede
And hir that is so faire and rede,
    Lufamour the brighte!"

Then the Kyng Arthour
And the Lady Lufamour
And all that were in the towre
    Graunted therwith.
Thay called Percevell the wight;
The Kyng doubbed hym to knyghte.
Thofe he couthe littill insighte,
    The childe was of pith.
He bad he solde be to prayse,
Therto hende and curtayse;
Sir Percevell the Galayse
    Thay called hym in kythe.
Kyng Arthour in Maydenlande
Dubbid hym knyghte with his hande,
Bad hym ther he his fo fande
    To gyff hym no grythe.

Grith takes he nane:
He rydes agayne the Sowdane
That highte Gollerotherame,
    That felle was in fighte.
In the felde so brade,
No more carpynge thay made,
Bot sone togedir thay rade,
    Theire schaftes to righte.
Gollerotheram, thofe he wolde wede,

Percevell bere hym fro his stede
Two londis one brede,
  With maystry and myghte.
At the erthe the Sowdane lay;
His stede gun rynn away;
Than said Percevell one play,
  "Thou haste that I the highte."

He sayd, "I highte the a dynt,
And now, me thynke, thou hase it hynt.
And I may, als I hafe mynt,
  Thou schalt it never mende."
Appon the Sowdan he duelled
To the grownde ther he was felled,
And to the erthe he hym helde
  With his speres ende.
Fayne wolde he hafe hym slayne,
This uncely Sowdane,
Bot gate couthe he get nane,
  So ill was he kende.
Than thynkes the childe
Of olde werkes full wylde:
"Hade I a fire now in this filde,
  Righte here he solde be brende."

He said, "Righte here I solde the brene,
And thou ne solde never more then
Fighte for no wymman,
  So I solde the fere!"
Then said Wawayne the knyghte,
"Thou myghte, and thou knewe righte,

And thou woldes of thi stede lighte,
   Wynn hym one were."
The childe was of gamen gnede;
Now he thynkes one thede,
"Lorde! whethir this be a stede
   I wende had bene a mere?"
In stede righte there he in stode,
He ne wiste nother of evyll ne gude,
Bot then chaunged his mode
   And slaked his spere.

When his spere was up tane,
Then gan this Gollerothiram,
This ilke uncely Sowdane,
   One his fete to gete.
Than his swerde drawes he,
Strykes at Percevell the fre.
The childe hadd no powsté
   His laykes to lett.
The stede was his awnn will:
Saw the swerde come hym till,
Leppe up over an hill,
   Fyve stryde mett.
Als he sprent forby,
The Sowdan keste up a cry;
The childe wann owt of study
   That he was inn sett.

Now ther he was in sett,
Owt of study he gett,
And lightis downn, withowtten lett,

Agaynes hym to goo.
He says, "Now hase thou taughte me
How that I sall wirke with the."
Than his swerde drawes he
   And strake to hym thro.
He hitt hym even one the nekk-bane,
Thurgh ventale and pesane.
The hede of the Sowdane
   He strykes the body fra.
Then full wightly he yode
To his stede, there he stode;
The milde mayden in mode,
   Mirthe may scho ma!

Many mirthes then he made;
In to the castell he rade,
And boldly he there habade
   With that mayden brighte.
Fayne were thay ilkane
That he had slane the Sowdane
And wele wonn that wymman,
   With maystry and myghte.
Thay said Percevell the yyng
Was beste worthy to be kyng,
For wele withowtten lesyng
   He helde that he highte.
Ther was no more for to say,
Bot sythen, appon that other day,
He weddys Lufamour the may,
   This Percevell the wighte.

Now hase Percevell the wight
Wedded Lufamour the bright,
And is a kyng full righte
   Of alle that lande brade.
Than Kyng Arthour in hy
Wolde no lengare ther ly:
Toke lefe at the lady.
   Fro tham than he rade:
Left Percevell the yyng
Off all that lande to be kyng,
For he had with a ryng
   The mayden that it hade.
Sythen, appon the tother day,
The Kyng went on his way,
The certane sothe, als I say,
   Withowtten any bade.

Now than yong Percevell habade
In those borowes so brade
For hir sake, that he hade
   Wedd with a ryng.
Wele weldede he that lande,
Alle bowes to his honde;
The folke, that he byfore fonde,
   Knewe hym for kyng.
Thus he wonnes in that wone
Till that the twelmonthe was gone,
With Lufamour his lemman.
   He thoghte on no thyng,
Now on his moder that was,

How scho levyde with the gres,
With more drynke and lesse,
　In welles, there thay spryng.

Drynkes of welles, ther thay spryng,
And gresse etys, withowt lesyng!
Scho liffede with none othir thyng
　In the holtes hare.
Till it byfelle appon a day,
Als he in his bedd lay,
Till hymselfe gun he say,
　Syghande full sare,
"The laste Yole-day that was,
Wilde wayes I chese:
My modir all manles
　Leved I thare."
Than righte sone saide he,
"Blythe sall I never be
Or I may my modir see,
　And wete how scho fare."

Now to wete how scho fare,
The knyght busked hym yare;
He wolde no lengare duelle thare
　For noghte that myghte bee.
Up he rose in that haulle,
Tuke his lefe at tham alle,
Both at grete and at smalle;
　Fro thaym wendis he.
Faire scho prayed hym even than,
Lufamour, his lemman,

Till the heghe dayes of Yole were gane,
  With hir for to bee.
Bot it served hir of no thyng:
A preste he made forthe bryng,
Hym a messe for to syng,
  And aftir rode he.

Now fro tham gun he ryde;
Ther wiste no man that tyde
Whedirwarde he wolde ryde,
  His sorowes to amende.
Forthe he rydes allone;
Fro tham he wolde everichone:
Mighte no man with hym gone,
  Ne whedir he wolde lende.
Bot forthe thus rydes he ay,
The certen sothe als I yow say,
Till he come at a way
  By a wode-ende.
Then herde he faste hym by
Als it were a woman cry:
Scho prayed to mylde Mary
  Som socoure hir to sende.

Scho sende hir socour full gude,
Mary, that es mylde of mode.
As he come thurgh the wode,
  A ferly he fande.
A birde, brighteste of ble,
Stode faste bonden till a tre -
I say it yow certanly -

Bothe fote and hande.
Sone askede he who,
When he sawe hir tho,
That had served hir so,
   That lady in lande.
Scho said, "Sir, the Blake Knyghte
Solde be my lorde with righte;
He hase me thusgates dighte
   Here for to stande."

She says, "Here mon I stande
For a faute that he fande
That sall I warande
   Is my moste mone.
Now to the I sall say:
Appon my bedd I lay
Appon the laste Yole-day -
   Twelve monethes es gone -
Were he knyghte, were he king,
He come one his playnge.
With me he chaungede a ring,
   The richeste of one.
The body myght I noghte see
That made that chaungyng with me,
Bot what that ever he be,
   The better hase he tone!"

Scho says, "The better hase he tane;
Siche a vertue es in the stane,
In alle this werlde wote I nane
   Siche stone in a rynge;

A man that had it in were
One his body for to bere,
There scholde no dyntys hym dere,
    Ne to the dethe brynge."
And then wiste Sir Percevale
Full wele by the ladys tale
That he had broghte hir in bale
    Thurgh his chaungyng.
Than also sone sayd he
To that lady so fre,
"I sall the louse fro the tre,
    Als I ame trewe kyng."

He was bothe kyng and knyght:
Wele he helde that he highte;
He loused the lady so brighte,
    Stod bown to the tre.
Down satt the lady,
And yong Percevall hir by.
Forwaked was he wery:
    Rist hym wolde he.
He wende wele for to ryst,
Bot it wolde nothyng laste.
Als he lay althir best,
    His hede one hir kne,
Scho putt on Percevell wighte,
Bad hym fle with all his myghte,
"For yonder comes the Blake Knyghte;
    Dede mon ye be!"

Scho sayd, "Dede mon ye be,

I say yow, sir certanly:
Yonder out comes he
   That will us bothe slee!"
The knyghte gan hir answere,
"Tolde ye me noghte lang ere
Ther solde no dynttis me dere,
   Ne wirke me no woo?"
The helme on his hede he sett;
Bot or he myght to his stede get,
The Blak Knyght with hym mett,
   His maistrys to mo.
He sayd, "How! hase thou here
Fonden now thi play-fere?
Ye schall haby it full dere
   Er that I hethen go!"

He said, "Or I hethyn go,
I sall sle yow bothe two,
And all siche othir mo,
   Thaire waryson to yelde."
Than sayd Percevell the fre,
"Now sone than sall we see
Who that es worthy to bee
   Slayne in the felde."
No more speke thay that tyde,
Bot sone togedir gan thay ryde,
Als men that wolde were habyde,
   With schafte and with schelde.
Than Sir Percevell the wight
Bare down the Blake Knyght.
Than was the lady so bright

His best socour in telde;

Scho was the beste of his belde:
Bot scho had there bene his schelde,
He had bene slayne in the felde,
   Right certeyne in hy.
Ever als Percevell the kene
Sold the knyghtis bane hafe bene,
Ay went the lady bytwene
   And cryed, "Mercy!"
Than the lady he forbere,
And made the Blak Knyghte to swere
Of alle evylls that there were,
   Forgiffe the lady.
And Percevell made the same othe
That he come never undir clothe
To do that lady no lothe
   That pendid to velany.

"I did hir never no velany;
Bot slepande I saw hir ly:
Than kist I that lady -
   I will it never layne.
I tok a ryng that I fande;
I left hir, I undirstande,
That sall I wele warande,
   Anothir ther-agayne."
Thofe it were for none other thyng,
He swere by Jhesu, Heven-kyng,
To wete withowtten lesyng,
   And here to be slayne;

"And all redy is the ryng;
And thou will myn agayne bryng,
Here will I make the chaungyng,
   And of myn awnn be fayne."

He saise, "Of myn I will be fayne."
The Blak Knyghte ansuers agayne:
Sayd, "For sothe, it is noghte to layne,
   Thou come over-late.
Als sone als I the ryng fande,
I toke it sone off hir hande;
To the lorde of this lande
   I bare it one a gate.
That gate with grefe hafe I gone:
I bare it to a gude mone,
The stalwortheste geant of one
   That any man wate.
Es it nowther knyghte ne kyng
That dorste aske hym that ryng,
That he ne wolde hym down dyng
   With harmes full hate."

"Be thay hate, be thay colde,"
Than said Percevell the bolde,
For the tale that he tolde
   He wex all tene.
He said, "Heghe on galous mote he hyng
That to the here giffes any ryng,
Bot thou myn agayne brynge,
   Thou haste awaye geven!
And yif it may no nother be,

Righte sone than tell thou me
The sothe: whilke that es he
    Thou knawes, that es so kene?
Ther es no more for to say,
Bot late me wynn it yif I may,
For thou hase giffen thi part of bothe away,
    Thof thay had better bene."

He says, "Thofe thay had better bene."
The knyghte ansuerde in tene,
"Thou sall wele wete, withowtten wene,
    Wiche that es he!
If thou dare do als thou says,
Sir Percevell de Galays,
In yone heghe palays,
    Therin solde he be,
The riche ryng with that grym!
The stane es bright and nothyng dym;
For sothe, ther sall thou fynd hym:
    I toke it fro me;
Owthir within or withowt,
Or one his play ther abowte,
Of the he giffes littill dowte,
    And that sall thou see."

He says, "That sall thou see,
I say the full sekirly."
And than forthe rydis he
    Wondirly swythe.
The geant stode in his holde,
That had those londis in wolde:

Saw Percevell, that was bolde,
   One his lande dryfe;
He calde one his portere:
   "How-gate may this fare?
I se a bolde man yare
   On my lande ryfe.
Go reche me my playlome,
And I sall go to hym sone;
Hym were better hafe bene at Rome,
   So ever mote I thryfe!"

Whethir he thryfe or he the,
Ane iryn clobe takes he;
Agayne Percevell the fre
   He went than full right.
The clobe wheyhed reghte wele
That a freke myght it fele:
The hede was of harde stele,
   Twelve stone weghte!
Ther was iryn in the wande,
Ten stone of the lande,
And one was byhynde his hande,
   For holdyng was dight.
Ther was thre and twenty in hale;
Full evyll myght any men smale,
That men telles nowe in tale,
   With siche a lome fighte.

Now are thay bothe bown,
Mett one a more brown,
A mile withowt any town,

Boldly with schelde.
Than saide the geant so wight,
Als sone als he sawe the knyght,
"Mahown, loved be thi myght!"
   And Percevell byhelde.
"Art thou hym, that," saide he than,
"That slew Gollerothirame?
I had no brothir bot hym ane,
   When he was of elde."
Than said Percevell the fre,
"Thurgh grace of God so sall I the,
And siche geantes as ye
   Sle thaym in the felde!"

Siche metyng was seldom sene.
The dales dynned thaym bytwene
For dynttis that thay gaffe bydene
   When thay so mett.
The gyant with his clobe-lome
Wolde hafe strekyn Percevell sone,
Bot he therunder wightely come,
   A stroke hym to sett.
The geant missede of his dynt;
The clobe was harde as the flynt:
Or he myght his staffe stynt
   Or his strengh lett,
The clobe in the erthe stode:
To the midschafte it wode.
The Percevell the gode,
   Hys swerde owt he get.

By then hys swerde owt he get,

  Strykes the geant withowtten lett,

Merkes even to his nekk,

    Reght even ther he stode;

His honde he strykes hym fro,

His lefte fote also,

With siche dyntis as tho.

    Nerre hym he yode.

Then sayd Percevell, "I undirstande

Thou myghte with a lesse wande

Hafe weledid better thi hande

    And hafe done the some gode;

Now bese it never for ane

The clobe of the erthe tane.

I tell thi gatis alle gane, In the tyme of Arthur an aunter bytydde,

  By the Turne Wathelan, as the boke telles,

Whan he to Carlele was comen, that conquerour kydde,

With dukes and dussiperes that with the dere dwelles.

To hunte at the herdes that longe had ben hydde,

On a day thei hem dight to the depe delles,

To fall of the femailes in forest were frydde,

Fayre by the fermesones in frithes and felles.

Thus to wode arn thei went, the wlonkest in wedes,

Bothe the Kyng and the Quene,

And al the doughti bydene.

Sir Gawayn, gayest on grene,

Dame Gaynour he ledes.

Thus Sir Gawayn the gay Gaynour he ledes,

In a gleterand gide that glemed full gay -

With riche ribaynes reversset, ho so right redes,
Rayled with rybees of riall array;
Her hode of a hawe huwe, ho that here hede hedes,
Of pillour, of palwerk, of perré to pay;
Schurde in a short cloke that the rayne shedes,
Set over with saffres sothely to say,
With saffres and seladynes set by the sides;
Here sadel sette of that ilke,
Saude with sambutes of silke;
On a mule as the mylke,
Gaili she glides.

Al in gleterand golde, gayly ho glides
The gates with Sir Gawayn, bi the grene welle.
And that burne on his blonke with the Quene bides
That borne was in Borgoyne, by boke and by belle.
He ladde that Lady so longe by the lawe sides;
Under a lorre they light, loghe by a felle.
And Arthur with his erles ernestly rides,
To teche hem to her tristres, the trouthe for to telle.
To here tristres he hem taught, ho the trouthe trowes.
Eche lorde withouten lette
To an oke he hem sette,
With bowe and with barselette,
Under the bowes.

Under the bowes thei bode, thes burnes so bolde,
To byker at thes baraynes in bonkes so bare.
There might hatheles in high herdes beholde,
Herken huntyng in hast, in holtes so hare.
Thei kest of here couples in cliffes so colde,

Conforte her kenettes to kele hem of care.

Thei fel of the femayles ful thikfolde;

With fressh houndes and fele, thei folowen her fare.

. . . .

With gret questes and quelles,

Both in frethes and felles.

All the dure in the delles,

Thei durken and dare.

Then durken the dere in the dymme skuwes,

That for drede of the deth droupes the do.

And by the stremys so strange that swftly swoghes

Thai werray the wilde and worchen hem wo.

The huntes thei halowe, in hurstes and huwes,

And till thaire riste raches relyes on the ro.

They gaf to no gamon grythe that on grounde gruwes.

The grete greundes in the greves so glady thei go;

So gladly thei gon in greves so grene.

The King blowe rechas

And folowed fast on the tras

With many sergeant of mas,

That solas to sene.

With solas thei semble, the pruddest in palle,

And suwen to the Soverayne within schaghes schene.

Al but Sir Gawayn, gayest of all,

Beleves with Dame Gaynour in greves so grene.

By a lorer ho was light, undur a lefesale

Of box and of berber bigged ful bene.

Fast byfore undre this ferly con fall

And this mekel mervaile that I shal of mene.

Now wol I of this mervaile mele, if I mote.

The day wex als dirke

As hit were mydnight myrke;

Thereof the King was irke

And light on his fote.

Thus to fote ar thei faren, the frekes unfayn,

And fleen fro the forest to the fawe felle.

Thay ranne faste to the roches, for reddoure of the raynne

For the sneterand snawe snartly hem snelles.

There come a lowe one the loughe - in londe is not to layne -

In the lyknes of Lucyfere, laytheste in Helle,

And glides to Sir Gawayn the gates to gayne,

Yauland and yomerand, with many loude yelle.

Hit yaules, hit yameres, with waymynges wete,

And seid, with siking sare,

"I ban the body me bare!

Alas! Now kindeles my care;

I gloppen and I grete!"

Then gloppenet and grete Gaynour the gay

And seid to Sir Gawen, "What is thi good rede?"

"Hit ar the clippes of the son, I herd a clerk say,"

And thus he confortes the Quene for his knighthede.

"Sir Cadour, Sir Clegis, Sir Costardyne, Sir Cay -

Thes knyghtes arn uncurtays, by Crosse and by Crede,

That thus oonly have me laft on my dethday

With the grisselist goost that ever herd I grede."

"Of the goost," quod the grome, "greve you no mare,

For I shal speke with the sprete.

And of the wayes I shall wete,

What may the bales bete
Of the bodi bare."

Bare was the body and blak to the bone,
Al biclagged in clay uncomly cladde.
Hit waried, hit wayment as a woman,
But on hide ne on huwe no heling hit hadde.
Hit stemered, hit stonayde, hit stode as a stone,
Hit marred, hit memered, hit mused for madde.
Agayn the grisly goost Sir Gawayn is gone;
He rayked oute at a res, for he was never drad.
Drad was he never, ho so right redes.
On the chef of the cholle,
A pade pikes on the polle,
With eighen holked ful holle
That gloed as the gledes.

Al glowed as a glede the goste there ho glides,
Umbeclipped in a cloude of clethyng unclere,
Serkeled with serpentes all aboute the sides -
To tell the todes theron my tonge wer full tere.
The burne braides oute the bronde, and the body bides;
Therefor the chevalrous knight changed no chere.
The houndes highen to the holtes, and her hede hides,
For the grisly goost made a grym bere.
The grete greundes wer agast of the grym bere.
The birdes in the bowes,
That on the goost glowes,
Thei skryke in the skowes
That hatheles may here.

Hathelese might here, the hendeste in halle,
How chatered the cholle, the chaftis and the chynne.
Then conjured the knight - on Crist con he calle:
"As thou was crucifiged on Croys to clanse us of syn:
That thou sei me the sothe whether thou shalle,
And whi thou walkest thes wayes the wodes within."
"I was of figure and face fairest of alle,
Cristened and knowen with kinges in my kynne;
I have kinges in my kyn knowen for kene.
God has me geven of his grace
To dre my paynes in this place.
I am comen in this cace
To speke with your Quene.

"Quene was I somwile, brighter of browes
Then Berell or Brangwayn, thes burdes so bolde;
Of al gamen or gle that on grounde growes
Gretter then Dame Gaynour, of garson and golde,
Of palaies, of parkes, of pondes, of plowes,
Of townes, of toures, of tresour untolde,
Of castelles, of contreyes, of cragges, of clowes.
Now am I caught oute of kide to cares so colde;
Into care am I caught and couched in clay.
Lo, sir curtays kniyght,
How delfulle deth has me dight!
Lete me onys have a sight
Of Gaynour the gay."

After Gaynour the gay Sir Gawyn is gon,
And to the body he her brought, the burde bright.
"Welcom, Waynour, iwis, worthi in won.

Lo, how delful deth has thi dame dight!

I was radder of rode then rose in the ron,

My ler as the lelé lonched on hight.

Now am I a graceles gost, and grisly I gron;

With Lucyfer in a lake logh am I light.

Thus am I lyke to Lucefere: takis witnes by mee!

For al thi fressh foroure,

Muse on my mirrour;

For, king and emperour,

Thus dight shul ye be.

"Thus dethe wil you dight, thare you not doute;

Thereon hertly take hede while thou art here.

Whan thou art richest arraied and ridest in thi route,

Have pité on the poer - thou art of power.

Burnes and burdes that ben the aboute,

When thi body is bamed and brought on a ber,

Then lite wyn the light that now wil the loute,

For then the helpes no thing but holy praier.

The praier of poer may purchas the pes -

Of that thou yeves at the yete,

Whan thou art set in thi sete,

With al merthes at mete

And dayntés on des.

"With riche dayntés on des thi diotes ar dight,

And I, in danger and doel, in dongone I dwelle,

Naxte and nedefull, naked on night.

Ther folo me a ferde of fendes of helle;

They hurle me unhendely; thei harme me in hight;

In bras and in brymston I bren as a belle.

Was never wrought in this world a wofuller wight.
Hit were ful tore any tonge my turment to telle;
Nowe wil Y of my turment tel or I go.
Thenk hertly on this -
Fonde to mende thi mys.
Thou art warned ywys:
Be war be my wo."

"Wo is me for thi wo," quod Waynour, "ywys!
But one thing wold I wite, if thi wil ware:
If auther matens or Mas might mende thi mys,
Or eny meble on molde? My merthe were the mare
If bedis of bisshopps might bring the to blisse,
Or coventes in cloistre might kere the of care.
If thou be my moder, grete mervaile hit is
That al thi burly body is broughte to be so bare!"
"I bare the of my body; what bote is hit I layn?
I brak a solempne avowe,
And no man wist hit but thowe;
By that token thou trowe,
That sothely I sayn."

"Say sothely what may the saven of thi sytis
And I shal make sere men to singe for thi sake.
But the baleful bestes that on thi body bites
Al blendis my ble - thi bones arn so blake!"
"That is luf paramour, listes and delites
That has me light and laft logh in a lake.
Al the welth of the world, that awey witis
With the wilde wormes that worche me wrake;
Wrake thei me worchen, Waynour, iwys.

Were thritty trentales don
Bytwene under and non,
Mi soule were socoured with son
And brought to the blys."

"To blisse bring the the Barne that bought the on Rode,
That was crucifiged on Croys and crowned with thorne.
As thou was cristened and crisomed with candel and code,
Folowed in fontestone on frely byforne -
Mary the mighti, myldest of mode,
Of whom the blisful barne in Bedlem was borne,
Lene me grace that I may grete the with gode
And mynge the with matens and Masses on morne."
"To mende us with Masses, grete myster hit were.
For Him that rest on the Rode,
Gyf fast of thi goode
To folke that failen the fode
While thou art here."

"Here hertly my honde thes hestes to holde,
With a myllion of Masses to make the mynnyng.
Bot one word," quod Waynour, "yit weten I wolde:
What wrathed God most, at thi weting?"
"Pride with the appurtenaunce, as prophetez han tolde
Bifore the peple, apertly in her preching.
Hit beres bowes bitter: therof be thou bolde;
That makes burnes so boune to breke his bidding.
But ho his bidding brekes, bare thei ben of blys;
But thei be salved of that sare,
Er they hethen fare,
They mon weten of care,

Waynour, ywys."

"Wysse me," quod Waynour, "som wey, if thou wost,
What bedis might me best to the blisse bring?"
"Mekenesse and mercy, thes arn the moost;
And sithen have pité on the poer, that pleses Heven king.
Sithen charité is chef, and then is chaste,
And then almessedede aure al other thing.
Thes arn the graceful giftes of the Holy Goste
That enspires iche sprete withoute speling.
Of this spiritual thing spute thou no mare.
Als thou art Quene in thi quert,
Hold thes wordes in hert.
Thou shal leve but a stert;
Hethen shal thou fare."

"How shal we fare," quod the freke, "that fonden to fight,
And thus defoulen the folke on fele kinges londes,
And riches over reymes withouten eny right,
Wynnen worshipp in werre thorgh wightnesse of hondes?"
"Your King is to covetous, I warne the sir knight.
May no man stry him with strenght while his whele stondes.
Whan he is in his magesté, moost in his might,
He shal light ful lowe on the sesondes.
And this chivalrous Kinge chef shall a chaunce:
Falsely Fortune in fight,
That wonderfull wheelwryght,
Shall make lordes to light -
Take witnesse by Fraunce.

"Fraunce haf ye frely with your fight wonnen;

Freol and his folke, fey ar they leved.

Bretayne and Burgoyne al to you bowen,

And al the Dussiperes of Fraunce with your dyn deved.

Gyan may grete the werre was bigonen;

There ar no lordes on lyve in that londe leved.

Yet shal the riche Romans with you be aurronen,

And with the Rounde Table the rentes be reved;

Then shal a Tyber untrue tymber you tene.

Gete the, Sir Gawayn:

Turne the to Tuskayn.

For ye shul lese Bretayn

With a knight kene.

"This knight shal kenely croyse the crowne,

And at Carlele shal that comly be crowned as king.

That sege shal be sesede at a sesone

That myche baret and bale to Bretayn shal bring.

Hit shal in Tuskan be tolde of the treson,

And ye shullen turne ayen for the tydynge.

Ther shal the Rounde Table lese the renoune:

Beside Ramsey ful rad at a riding

In Dorsetshire shal dy the doughtest of alle.

Gete the, Sir Gawayn,

The boldest of Bretayne;

In a slake thou shal be slayne,

Sich ferlyes shull falle.

"Suche ferlies shull fal, withoute eny fable,

Uppon Cornewayle coost with a knight kene.

Sir Arthur the honest, avenant and able,

He shal be wounded, iwys - wothely, I wene.

And al the rial rowte of the Rounde Table,
Thei shullen dye on a day, the doughty bydene,
Suppriset with a suget: he beris hit in sable,
With a sauter engreled of silver full shene.
He beris hit of sable, sothely to say;
In riche Arthures halle,
The barne playes at the balle
That outray shall you alle,
Delfully that day.

"Have gode day, Gaynour, and Gawayn the gode;
I have no lenger tome tidinges to telle.
I mot walke on my wey thorgh this wilde wode
In my wonyngstid in wo for to welle.
Fore Him that rightwisly rose and rest on the Rode,
Thenke on the danger and the dole that I yn dwell.
Fede folke for my sake that failen the fode
And menge me with matens and Masse in melle.
Masses arn medecynes to us that bale bides;
Us thenke a Masse as swete
As eny spice that ever ye yete."
With a grisly grete
The goste awey glides.

With a grisly grete the goost awey glides
And goes with gronyng sore thorgh the greves grene.
The wyndes, the weders, the welken unhides -
Then unclosed the cloudes, the son con shene.
The King his bugle has blowen and on the bent bides;
His fare folke in the frith, thei flokken bydene,
And al the riall route to the Quene rides;

She sayes hem the selcouthes that thei hadde ther seen.
The wise of the weder, forwondred they were.
Prince proudest in palle,
Dame Gaynour and alle,
Went to Rondoles Halle
To the suppere.

The King to souper is set, served in sale,
Under a siller of silke dayntly dight
With al worshipp and wele, innewith the walle,
Briddes brauden and brad in bankers bright.
There come in a soteler with a symballe,
A lady lufsom of lote ledand a knight;
Ho raykes up in a res bifor the Rialle
And halsed Sir Arthur hendly on hight.
Ho said to the Soverayne, wlonkest in wede,
"Mon makeles of might,
Here commes an errant knight.
Do him reson and right
For thi manhede."

The mon in his mantell sittes at his mete
In pal pured to pay, prodly pight,
Trofelyte and traverste with trewloves in trete;
The tasses were of topas that wer thereto tight.
He gliffed up with his eighen that grey wer and grete,
With his beveren berde, on that burde bright.
He was the soveraynest of al sitting in sete
That ever segge had sen with his eye sight.
King crowned in kith carpes hir tille:
"Welcom, worthely wight -

He shal have reson and right!
Whethen is the comli knight,
If hit be thi wille?"

Ho was the worthiest wight that eny wy welde wolde;
Here gide was glorious and gay, of a gresse grene.
Here belle was of blunket, with birdes ful bolde,
Brauded with brende gold, and bokeled ful bene.
Here fax in fyne perré was fretted in folde,
Contrefelet and kelle coloured full clene,
With a crowne craftly al of clene golde.
Here kercheves were curiouse with many proude prene,
Her perré was praysed with prise men of might:
Bright birdes and bolde
Had ynoghe to beholde
Of that frely to folde,
And on the hende knight.

The knight in his colours was armed ful clene,
With his comly crest clere to beholde,
His brené and his basnet burneshed ful bene,
With a bordur abought al of brende golde.
His mayles were mylke white, enclawet ful clene;
His horse trapped of that ilke, as true men me tolde;
His shelde on his shulder of silver so shene,
With bere hedes of blake browed ful bolde;
His horse in fyne sandel was trapped to the hele.
And, in his cheveron biforne,
Stode as an unicorne,
Als sharp as a thorne,
An anlas of stele.

In stele he was stuffed, that stourne uppon stede,
Al of sternes of golde, that stanseld was one straye;
His gloves, his gamesons glowed as a glede
With graynes of rebé that graithed ben gay.
And his schene schynbaudes, that sharp wer to shrede,
His poleinus with pelydodis were poudred to pay.
With a launce on loft that lovely con lede;
A freke on a freson him folowed, in fay.
The freson was afered for drede of that fare,
For he was selden wonte to se
The tablet fluré:
Siche gamen ne gle
Sagh he never are.

Arthur asked on hight, herand him alle:
"What woldes thou, wee, if hit be thi wille?
Tel me what thou seches and whether thou shalle,
And whi thou, sturne on thi stede, stondes so stille?"
He wayved up his viser fro his ventalle;
With a knightly contenaunce, he carpes him tille:
"Whether thou be cayser or king, her I the becalle
Fore to finde me a freke to fight with my fille.
Fighting to fraist I fonded fro home."
Then seid the King uppon hight,
"If thou be curteys knight,
Late and lenge al nyght,
And tel me thi nome."

"Mi name is Sir Galaron, withouten eny gile,
The grettest of Galwey of greves and gyllis,

Of Connok, of Conyngham, and also Kyle,
Of Lomond, of Losex, of Loyan hilles.
Thou has wonen hem in werre with a wrange wile
And geven hem to Sir Gawayn - that my hert grylles.
But he shal wring his honde and warry the wyle,
Er he weld hem, ywys, agayn myn unwylles.
Bi al the welth of the worlde, he shal hem never welde,
While I the hede may bere,
But if he wyn hem in were,
With a shelde and a spere,
On a faire felde.

"I wol fight on a felde - thereto I make feith -
With eny freke uppon folde that frely is borne.
To lese suche a lordshipp me wolde thenke laith,
And iche lede opon lyve wold lagh me to scorne."
"We ar in the wode went to walke on oure waith,
To hunte at the hertes with hounde and with horne.
We ar in oure gamen; we have no gome graithe,
But yet thou shalt be mached be mydday tomorne.
Forthi I rede the, thenke rest al night."
Gawayn, grathest of all,
Ledes him oute of the hall
Into a pavilion of pall
That prodly was pight.

Pight was it prodly with purpour and palle,
Birdes brauden above, in brend gold bright.
Inwith was a chapell, a chambour, a halle,
A chymné with charcole to chaufe the knight.
His stede was stabled and led to the stalle;

Hay hertly he had in haches on hight.

Sithen thei braide up a borde, and clothes thei calle,

Sanapes and salers, semly to sight,

Torches and brochetes and stondardes bitwene.

Thus thei served that knight

And his worthely wight,

With rich dayntes dight

In silver so shene.

In silver so semely thei served of the best,

With vernage in veres and cuppes ful clene.

And thus Sir Gawayn the good glades hour gest,

With riche dayntees endored in disshes bydene.

Whan the riall renke was gone to his rest,

The King to counsaile has called his knightes so kene.

"Loke nowe, lordes, oure lose be not lost.

Ho shal encontre with the knight? Kestes you bitwene."

Then seid Gawayn the goode, "Shal hit not greve.

Here my honde I you hight,

I woll fight with the knight

In defence of my right,

Lorde, by your leve."

"I leve wel," quod the King. "Thi lates ar light,

But I nolde for no lordeshipp se thi life lorne."

"Let go!" quod Sir Gawayn. "God stond with the right!

If he skape skathlesse, hit were a foule skorne."

In the daying of the day, the doughti were dight,

And herden matens and Masse erly on morne.

By that on Plumton Land a palais was pight,

Were never freke opon folde had foughten biforne.

Thei setten listes bylyve on the logh lande.

Thre soppes demayn

Thei brought to Sir Gawayn

For to confort his brayn,

The King gared commaunde.

The King commaunded kindeli the Erlis son of Kent:

"Curtaysly in this case, take kepe to the knight."

With riche dayntees or day he dyned in his tente;

After buskes him in a brené that burneshed was bright.

Sithen to Waynour wisly he went;

He laft in here warde his worthly wight.

After aither in high hour horses thei hent,

And at the listes on the lande lordely done light

Alle bot thes two burnes, baldest of blode.

The Kinges chaier is set

Abowve on a chacelet;

Many galiard gret

For Gawayn the gode.

Gawayn and Galerone gurden her stedes;

Al in gleterand golde, gay was here gere.

The lordes bylyve hom to list ledes,

With many serjant of mace, as was the manere.

The burnes broched the blonkes that the side bledis;

Ayther freke opon folde has fastned his spere.

Shaftes in shide wode thei shindre in shedes,

So jolilé thes gentil justed on were!

Shaftes thei shindre in sheldes so shene,

And sithen, with brondes bright,

Riche mayles thei right.

There encontres the knight
With Gawayn on grene.

Gawayn was gaily grathed in grene,
With his griffons of golde engreled full gay,
Trifeled with tranes and trueloves bitwene;
On a startand stede he strikes on stray.
That other in his turnaying, he talkes in tene:
"Whi drawes thou the on dregh and makes siche deray?"
He swapped him yn at the swyre with a swerde kene;
That greved Sir Gawayn to his dethday.
The dyntes of that doughty were doutwis bydene;
Fifté mayles and mo
The swerde swapt in two,
The canelbone also,
And clef his shelde shene.

He clef thorgh the cantell that covered the knight,
Thorgh the shinand shelde a shaftmon and mare.
And then the lathely lord lowe uppon hight,
And Gawayn greches therwith and gremed ful sare:
"I shal rewarde the thi route, if I con rede right."
He folowed in on the freke with a fressh fare;
Thorgh blason and brené, that burneshed wer bright,
With a burlich bronde thorgh him he bare.
The bronde was blody that burneshed was bright.
Then gloppened that gay -
Hit was no ferly, in fay.
The sturne strikes on stray
In stiropes stright.

Streyte in his steroppes, stoutely he strikes,
And waynes at Sir Wawayn als he were wode.
Then his lemman on lowde skirles and skrikes,
When that burly burne blenket on blode.
Lordes and ladies of that laike likes
And thonked God of his grace for Gawayn the gode.
With a swap of a swerde, that swithely him swykes;
He stroke of the stede hede streite there he stode.
The faire fole fondred and fel, bi the Rode.
Gawayn gloppened in hert;
He was swithely smert.
Oute of sterops he stert
Fro Grissell the goode.

"Grissell," quod Gawayn, "gon is, God wote!
He was the burlokest blonke that ever bote brede.
By Him that in Bedeleem was borne ever to ben our bote,
I shall venge the today, if I con right rede."
"Go fecche me my freson, fairest on fote;
He may stonde the in stoure in as mekle stede."
"No more for the faire fole then for a risshrote.
But for doel of the dombe best that thus shuld be dede,
I mourne for no montur, for I may gete mare."
Als he stode by his stede,
That was so goode at nede,
Ner Gawayn wax wede,
So wepputte he sare.

Thus wepus for wo Wowayn the wight,
And wenys him to quyte, that wonded is sare.
That other drogh him on dreght for drede of the knight

And boldely broched his blonk on the bent bare.

"Thus may thou dryve forthe the day to the derk night!"

The son was passed by that mydday and mare.

Within the listes the lede lordly done light;

Touard the burne with his bronde he busked him yare.

To bataile they bowe with brondes so bright.

Shene sheldes wer shred,

Bright brenés bybled;

Many doughti were adred,

So fersely thei fight.

Thus thei feght on fote on that fair felde

As fressh as a lyon that fautes the fille.

Wilelé thes wight men thair wepenes they welde;

Wyte ye wele, Sir Gawayn wantis no will.

He brouched him yn with his bronde under the brode shelde

Thorgh the waast of the body and wonded him ille.

The swerd stent for no stuf - hit was so wel steled.

That other startis on bak and stondis stonstille.

Though he were stonayed that stonde, he strikes ful sare -

He gurdes to Sir Gawayn

Thorgh ventaile and pesayn;

He wanted noght to be slayn

The brede of an hare.

Hardely then thes hathelese on helmes they hewe.

Thei beten downe beriles and bourdures bright;

Shildes on shildres that shene were to shewe,

Fretted were in fyne golde, thei failen in fight.

Stones of iral thay strenkel and strewe;

Stithe stapeles of stele they strike done stright.

Burnes bannen the tyme the bargan was brewe,
The doughti with dyntes so delfully were dight.
The dyntis of tho doghty were doutous bydene.
Bothe Sir Lete and Sir Lake
Miche mornyng thei make.
Gaynor gret for her sake
With her grey eyen.

Thus gretis Gaynour with bothe her grey yene
For gref of Sir Gawayn, grisly was wound.
The knight of corage was cruel and kene,
And, with a stele bronde, that sturne oft stound;
Al the cost of the knyght he carf downe clene.
Thorgh the riche mailes that ronke were and rounde
With a teneful touche he taght him in tene,
He gurdes Sir Galeron groveling on gronde.
Grisly on gronde, he groned on grene.
Als wounded as he was,
Sone unredely he ras
And folowed fast on his tras
With a swerde kene.

Kenely that cruel kevered on hight,
And with a cast of the carhonde in cantil he strikes,
And waynes at Sir Wawyn, that worthely wight.
But him lymped the worse, and that me wel likes.
He atteled with a slenk haf slayn him in slight;
The swerd swapped on his swange and on the mayle slikes,
And Gawayn bi the coler keppes the knight.
Then his lemman on loft skrilles and skrikes -
Ho gretes on Gaynour with gronyng grylle:

"Lady makeles of might,
Haf mercy on yondre knight
That is so delfull dight,
If hit be thi wille."

Than wilfully Dame Waynour to the King went;
Ho caught of her coronall and kneled him tille:
"As thou art Roye roial, richest of rent,
And I thi wife wedded at thi owne wille -
Thes burnes in the bataile so blede on the bent,
They arn wery, iwis, and wonded full ille.
Thorgh her shene sheldes, her shuldres ar shent;
The grones of Sir Gawayn dos my hert grille.
The grones of Sir Gawayne greven me sare.
Wodest thou leve, Lorde,
Make thes knightes accorde,
Hit were a grete conforde
For all that here ware."

Then spak Sir Galeron to Gawayn the good:
"I wende never wee in this world had ben half so wight.
Here I make the releyse, renke, by the Rode,
And, byfore thiese ryalle, resynge the my ryghte;
And sithen make the monraden with a mylde mode
As man of medlert makeles of might."
He talkes touard the King on hie ther he stode,
And bede that burly his bronde that burneshed was bright:
"Of rentes and richesse I make the releyse."
Downe kneled the knight
And carped wordes on hight;
The King stode upright

And commaunded pes.

The King commaunded pes and cried on hight,
And Gawayn was goodly and laft for his sake.
Then lordes to listes they lopen ful light -
Sir Ewayn Fiz Uryayn and Arrak Fiz Lake,
Marrake and Moylard, that most wer of might -
Bothe thes travayled men they truly up take.
Unneth might tho sturne stonde upright -
What, for buffetes and blode, her blees wex blak;
Her blees were brosed, for beting of brondes.
Withouten more lettyng,
Dight was here saghtlyng;
Bifore the comly King,
Thei held up her hondes.

"Here I gif Sir Gawayn, with gerson and golde,
Al the Glamergan londe with greves so grene,
The worship of Wales at wil and at wolde,
With Criffones Castelles curnelled ful clene;
Eke Ulstur Halle to hafe and to holde,
Wayford and Waterforde, wallede I wene;
Two baronrees in Bretayne with burghes so bolde,
That arn batailed abought and bigged ful bene.
I shal doue the a duke and dubbe the with honde,
Withthi thou saghtil with the knight
That is so hardi and wight,
And relese him his right,
And graunte him his londe."

"Here I gif Sir Galeron," quod Gawayn, "withouten any gile,

Al the londes and the lithes fro Lauer to Layre,

Connoke and Carlele, Conyngham and Kile;

Yet, if he of chevalry chalange ham for aire,

The Lother, the Lemmok, the Loynak, the Lile,

With frethis and forestes and fosses so faire.

Withthi under our lordeship thou lenge here a while,

And to the Round Table make thy repaire,

I shal refeff the in felde in forestes so fair."

Bothe the King and the Quene

And al the doughti bydene,

Thorgh the greves so grene,

To Carlele thei cair.

The King to Carlele is comen with knightes so kene,

And al the Rounde Table on rial aray.

The wees that weren wounded so wothely, I wene,

Surgenes sone saned, sothely to say;

Bothe confortes the knightes, the King and the Quene.

Thei were dubbed dukes both on a day.

There he wedded his wife, wlonkest I wene,

With giftes and garsons, Sir Galeron the gay;

Thus that hathel in high withholdes that hende.

Whan he was saned sonde,

Thei made Sir Galeron that stonde

A knight of the Table Ronde

To his lyves ende.

Waynour gared wisely write into the west

To al the religious to rede and to singe;

Prestes with procession to pray were prest,

With a mylion of Masses to make the mynnynge.

Bokelered men, bisshops the best,

Thorgh al Bretayne belles the burde gared rynge.

This ferely bifelle in Ingulwud Forest,

Under a holte so hore at a huntyng -

Suche a huntyng in holtis is noght to be hide.

Thus to forest they fore,

Thes sterne knightes in store.

In the tyme of Arthore

This anter betide.

   Bi the gude Rode!"

He says, "By the gud Rode,

As evyll als thou ever yode,

Of thi fote thou getis no gode;

   Bot lepe if thou may!"

The geant gan the clobe lefe,

And to Percevell a dynt he yefe

In the nekk with his nefe.

   So ne neghede thay.

At that dynt was he tene:

He strikes off the hande als clene

Als ther hadde never none bene.

   That other was awaye.

Sythen his hede gan he off hafe;

He was ane unhende knave

A geantberde so to schafe,

   For sothe, als I say!

Now for sothe, als I say,

He lete hym ly there he lay,

And rydis forthe one his way

To the heghe holde.
The portare saw his lorde slayne;
The kayes durste he noght layne.
He come Percevell agayne;
    The gatis he hym yolde.
At the firste bygynnyng,
He askede the portere of the ryng -
If he wiste of it any thyng -
    And he hym than tolde:
He taughte hym sone to the kiste
Ther he alle the golde wiste,
Bade hym take what hym liste
    Of that he hafe wolde.

Percevell sayde, hafe it he wolde,
And schott owtt all the golde
Righte there appon the faire molde;
    The ryng owte glade.
The portare stode besyde,
Sawe the ryng owt glyde,
Sayde ofte, "Wo worthe the tyde
That ever was it made!"
Percevell answerde in hy,
And asked wherefore and why
He banned it so brothely,
    Bot if he cause hade.
Then alsone said he,
And sware by his lewté:
"The cause sall I tell the,
    Withowten any bade."

He says, "Withowtten any bade,
The knyghte that it here hade,
Theroff a presande he made,
   And hedir he it broghte.
Mi mayster tuke it in his hande,
Ressayved faire that presande:
He was chefe lorde of this lande,
   Als man that mekill moghte.
That tyme was here fast by
Wonnande a lady,
And hir wele and lely
   He luffede, als me thoghte.
So it byfelle appon a day,
Now the sothe als I sall say,
Mi lorde went hym to play,
   And the lady bysoghte.

Now the lady byseches he
That scho wolde his leman be;
Fast he frayned that free,
   For any kyns aughte.
At the firste bygynnyng,
He wolde hafe gyffen hir the ryng;
And when scho sawe the tokynyng,
   Then was scho un-saughte.
Scho gret and cried in hir mone;
Sayd, 'Thefe, hase thou my sone slone
And the ryng fro hym tone,
   That I hym bitaughte?'
Hir clothes ther scho rafe hir fro,
And to the wodd gan scho go;

Thus es the lady so wo,
   And this is the draghte.

For siche draghtis als this,
Now es the lady wode, iwys,
And wilde in the wodde scho es,
   Ay sythen that ilke tyde.
Fayne wolde I take that free,
Bot alsone als scho sees me,
Faste awaye dose scho flee:
   Will scho noghte abyde."
Then sayde Sir Percevell,
"I will assaye full snelle
To make that lady to duelle;
   Bot I will noghte ryde:
One my fete will I ga,
That faire lady to ta.
Me aughte to bryng hir of wa:
   I laye in hir syde."

He sayse, "I laye in hir syde;
I sall never one horse ryde
Till I hafe sene hir in tyde,
   Spede if I may;
Ne none armoure that may be
Sall come appone me
Till I my modir may see,
   Be nyghte or by day.
Bot reghte in the same wode
That I firste fro hir yode,
That sall be in my mode

Aftir myn other play;
Ne I ne sall never mare
Come owt of yone holtis hare
Till I wete how scho fare,
    For sothe, als I saye."

Now for sothe, als I say,
With that he helde one his way,
And one the morne, when it was day,
    Forthe gonn he fare.
His armour he leved therin,
Toke one hym a gayt-skynne,
And to the wodde gan he wyn,
    Among the holtis hare.
A sevenyght long hase he soghte;
His modir ne fyndis he noghte.
Of mete ne drynke he ne roghte,
    So full he was of care.
Till the nynte day, byfell
That he come to a welle
Ther he was wonte for to duelle
    And drynk take hym thare.

When he had dronken that tyde,
Forthirmare gan he glyde;
Than was he warre, hym besyde,
    Of the lady so fre;
Bot when scho sawe hym thare,
Scho bygan for to dare,
And sone gaffe hym answare,
    That brighte was of ble.

Scho bigan to call and cry:
Sayd, "Siche a sone hade I!"
His hert lightened in hy,
   Blythe for to bee.
Be that he come hir nere
That scho myght hym here,
He said, "My modir full dere,
   Wele byde ye me!"

Be that, so nere getis he
That scho myghte nangatis fle,
I say yow full certeynly.
   Hir byhoved ther to byde.
Scho stertis appon hym in tene;
Wete ye wele, withowtten wene,
Had hir myghte so mekill bene,
   Scho had hym slayne that tyde!
Bot his myghte was the mare,
And up he toke his modir thare;
One his bake he hir bare:
   Pure was his pryde.
To the castell, withowtten mare,
The righte way gon he fare;
The portare was redy yare,
   And lete hym in glyde.

In with his modir he glade,
Als he sayse that it made;
With siche clothes als thay hade,
   Thay happed hir forthy.

The geant had a drynk wroghte,
The portere sone it forthe broghte,
For no man was his thoghte
  Bot for that lady.
Thay wolde not lett long thon,
Bot lavede in hir with a spone.
Then scho one slepe fell also sone,
  Reght certeyne in hy.
Thus the lady there lyes
Thre nyghttis and thre dayes,
And the portere alwayes
  Lay wakande hir by.

Thus the portare woke hir by -
Ther whills hir luffed sekerly, -
Till at the laste the lady
  Wakede, als I wene.
Then scho was in hir awenn state
And als wele in hir gate
Als scho hadde nowthir arely ne late
  Never therowte bene.
Thay sett tham down one thaire kne,
Thanked Godde, alle three,
That he wolde so appon tham see
  As it was there sene.
Sythen aftir gan thay ta
A riche bathe for to ma,
And made the lady in to ga,
  In graye and in grene.

Than Sir Percevell in hy

Toke his modir hym by,

I say yow than certenly,

   And home went hee.

Grete lordes and the Qwene

Welcomed hym al bydene;

When thay hym on lyfe sene;

   Than blythe myghte thay bee.

Sythen he went into the Holy Londe,

Wanne many cités full stronge,

And there was he slayne, I undirstonde;

   Thusgatis endis hee.

Now Jhesu Criste, hevens Kyng,

Als He es Lorde of all thyng,

Grante us all His blyssyng!

   Amen, for charyté!

Quod Robert Thornton

Explicit Sir Percevell de Gales

Here endys the Romance of Sir Percevell of Gales, Cosyn to King Arthoure.

More Arthurian Legends

We'd love for you to join our community! For more Arthurian texts, resources, and fiction, visit some of the links below!

The Website

www.mythbank.com

Facebook

www.facebook.com/mythbank

Instagram

instagram.com/mythbankwebsite

Made in the USA
Las Vegas, NV
15 May 2024

89965661R00089